Ginetta Finds a Soul

Vampire Memoirs
Book 3

Nicola Ormerod

to the highest buyer. Mama got such a worried look on her face when she thought of it.

The day the soldiers came was a beautiful day. The sun was hot in the sky and my brothers and I ran wild about the farm playing hide and seek and making mud pies. When the screams started we were in one of the cattle barns. I ran and peered through the doorway to see a Roman soldier chasing a woman across the field. When he caught her he dragged her away by her hair. The screams were getting louder and there were more of them. I climbed up to the top of the hay pile with my two brothers and buried us all as best as I could. Jason was only five and he began to cry. I hugged him to me fiercely and tried to shush him. My other brother Julius was eight and he was being so brave he lay quietly but I could see tears streaming down his face.

"Check the barns and out houses." Came a deep rasping voice.

It was so near it made us all jump and Jason sobbed even harder.

"Hush Jason, please." I begged

"I want momma. I want momma" Came his shaky reply.

"Please just hush."

I remember that moment when the doors bust open. We ducked our heads down and I clamped a hand tightly over Jason's mouth. 'Please lord don't let them find us', I thought to myself. They did of course. Jason was sobbing against me hand they probably heard it the second the

Chapter One

I don't have a lot of childhood memories. I think of my childhood ended the day our village was ransacked and my family was captured and taken into slavery. I don't know the exact year because I was only ten years old at the time but it was around the time that Christ was born. Our village was small and my father was a prominent member of its community. We lived a happy, simple life, neither poor, nor rich but somewhere in between. I had two younger brothers and along with my beautiful mother we lived and worked on our cattle farm. As a young lady I spent my days helping my mother bake and clean and the boys usually followed our father around the farm. I had dreams of marriage and children the same as any young girl on the cusp of womanhood. It wasn't uncommon to be married at twelve or thirteen.

Word had reached our village about soldiers from Rome ransacking small towns and capturing all able-bodied people for slavery. I remember thinking that it would be horrible to go through such a thing but my young mind could not comprehend the reality of it and besides you never think such bad things will happen to your family. The people were simply rounded up, chained and carted off to Rome and sold

Works by Nicola Ormerod from Vamptasy Publishing:

The Vampire Memoirs:
Red's Robin
The Taming of Ilona
Ginetta Finds a Soul

For my Mum,
Beauty and Grace
Silent and Firm
Loving and Respected
Missed every day.

entered the barn. They lifted Julius by the hair and he kicked and screamed. Then they tried to take Jason but he clung on fast and I wasn't going to let go either. I screamed at them to let us go but they ignored us. We were separated. My two brothers were dragged off in one direction and I was dragged toward the centre of the village.

They had rounded up all the women and tied them to several carts. I saw mamma and I finally broke free and ran to her. I fell and grabbed her stolla sobbing.

"They took the boys mamma."

"Oh honey." She sobbed back just as hard.

The soldier had caught back up with me and tied my hands with a long length of rope. He was just about to tie me to the cart beside my mother when another soldier stopped him.

"We could have some fun with that one." He grinned and winked at him.

"Please no…" My mother started

Much to my surprise the soldier received a back hander from the other.

"Are you sick?" The first replied. "I have a daughter her age"

"Ssssorrry, sir"

"Get out of my sight, and you leave this one alone."

I breathed a sigh of relief.

"What's happening mamma?" I asked when I was bound next to her and the men had gone.

"I don't know honey but at least we are together."

As soon as everyone was rounded up we squashed into the carts and our journey began. It seemed we travelled for miles, darkness fell and I slept. I woke in my mother's arms and the sun was just rising in the sky. She looked exhausted. Her beautiful raven hair matted with sweat and dirt and her stolla, once a clean cream was smudged with grime.

We were taken to Rome into a large open cobbled square. Then the citizens of Rome began parading in and looking round all the women that had been captured. Cheeks were pinched and people, human beings were poked and prodded like cattle. Soon haggling began and then some women were led off to their new homes.

"Are they selling us mamma?"

"Yes honey."

"We will escape?" I said determined

"Not likely sweetheart just stay close to me."

A large sweaty man with greasy grey hair came over and eyed up my mother.

"How much for the dark haired one?" He shouted to a plain clothed man nearby.

"For her," He said approaching us, "she is a lovely woman. 3000D

"That's too much."

"Please sir," My mother stammered to the grey haired man. "My daughter, please don't separate us."

The man looked down at us then he curled his lip.

"I have no use for a child." He barked.

"Ah but in a few years she will have her uses I'm sure." The plain clothed man urged.

"Hmm true…" He scratched his huge belly as he pondered what to do. " I will give you 3000 for both."

"Deal." He untied us and the money was exchanged.

I huddled close to mum and she held her arms around me protectively. Our new owner eyed us up and down.

"Now then I wasn't banking on escorting two home and I don't want any runaways so…" he grabbed my wrist and yanked me to him. "I think I'll hold on to the little one."

"You won't get any trouble from us sir, please don't hurt her." My mother kept her head down as she spoke.

He dragged me a short way through the busy streets of Rome with my mother following closely behind. When she saw me starting to sob she shook her head quickly. I think she realised that our owner didn't want me in the first place and if I were a nuisance then he would probably sell me on.

We arrived at a medium sized villa, larger than our home but a lot shabbier. Were we to be housekeepers for this old man? I might have only been ten but I knew I could impress him with my house keeping skills. I could cook basic broths and I could scrub linens clean. Mother had seen to it that from an early age I helped out where I could.

We were ushered to the basement door.

"Now missy," he pointed at my mother. "Drusilla downstairs will fill you in on everything you need to know. You will be tending to drinks for a few days and then put to work. Do you understand?"

My mother nodded.

"This is the only way in and out of the basement. If you disappear I will see that you are hunted down and strips of flesh torn from your body and then… I'll do the same to her." He pointed a fat hairy knuckled finger at me.

"Yes sir." My mother replied hastily

"Now go. Rest you start work in two hours. I want this little one to make herself useful if I get any trouble from her, she goes."

"Yes sir"

The door slammed shut and we heard the bolt sliding across, locking us inside. We made our way down the dark, slightly dank smelling stairs.

"Mama, what's going…?"

"Quiet just a second honey."

She took my hand and led us down the stairs. I could her women's laughter coming from one of the rooms and we followed it. It was a huge kitchen with a large fire and pot bubbling away. There were half a dozen roughly cut benches and about twenty women sat around. We waited in the doorway for our presence to be noticed. A dark haired woman finally saw us standing there and she clapped her hands together and smiled warmly. She had a head of black hair and dark olive skin. Her features were worn but beautiful.

"Augustus said he was going to the slave market today. Come in. Don't be scared, we don't bite. We save that for the clients."

Clients? Why would we bite clients? It wasn't my place to question adults so I remained silent.

"I'm Drusilla." The dark haired woman paused then took a look at me. "Dear lord, he's bought a child. I thought he could stoop no lower. He expects me to train a child for…"

"No." Mother interrupted. "This is my daughter Ginetta. He bought us as a package but instructed me to find her household tasks to do."

"Thank god. I take it you know about the work that you will be doing."

"Yes." My mother hung her head in shame.

"We are all in the same boat dear. All of us were wives and mothers only you are the only one of us that has been able to keep hold of our child."

A petite blond sat at one of the benches spoke up.

"If Augustus didn't want the little one in the first place I'll wager that he'll soon forget all about her, hell he can't even remember our names half the time."

"She's right," Drusilla said, "His memory is terrible. He sent Amelle to market twice for our food rations last week. We ate heartily." She laughed. "What's your name dear?"

"I'm Vianne"

"Pleased to meet you. Come sit down, eat. I only have one rule here. You don't run away. Augustus will lash me and he has for every slave that has run away. I'll add that all of them have been found and none of them are in this room. Ok"

"Yes"

"We will keep the little one well hidden so she will be safe ok."

"Thank you." My mother smiled.

I lived under the illusion that my mother was some sort of barmaid/house wife. I was a child and I had no idea about brothels and prostitutes and couldn't get my head around the fact that someone had simply come into the village and taken us. For the next few weeks I thought constantly about my father and brothers. My mother and I shared a small cot bed although it was usually dawn by the time she came to sleep and then I would get up and make myself useful. When I checked on my sleeping mother in between my chores she would talk in her sleep, whispering my father's name and tossing and turning. My tasks were simple and I carried them out well. I took the laundry left at the bottom of the cellar stairs to be scrubbed clean. I swept and I helped peel endless potatoes and ground wheat.

All the women that lived there were wonderful and I think they looked upon me as their own after a few weeks. I never saw our owner Augustus, he kept to nighttime hours and Drusilla said he never mentioned me at all.

Soon I was entrusted to go to market for supplies. Because most of the girls kept to odd night routines it made sense for me to be the one to go shopping and I was extremely excited about it. The market was nearby, only a two minute walk, so I was perfectly safe.

I set off, wicker basket in hand and made my first steps on my own into the big city. Rome was a magical sight then. With state of the art waterways, sewers and even public baths where you could bathe in water so hot it turned your skin red. I had only been sent for vegetables and some dried meat for a stew but I decided I would have a little look around. I had set off slightly later than I had intended and the sky was beginning to darken but winter was setting in fast so it was only early. I looked at all the delightful things I had never set eyes on before. Sugared fruit hanging from one stall made my mouth water and someone else selling exotic fruit that smelt divine. I bought some onions, carrots and dried beef and also some sweet bread that Drusilla loved. I was placing the change the stallholder had given me into my little purse when I caught sight of a man walking through the stalls. He looked like some kind of God to me. Standing taller than any man I had ever seen. He had short brown hair and he was wearing a toga of dark velvet Red with a gold trim. My young mind looked at him in complete awe. As he neared me I saw that his eyes were the brightest green and as he caught me looking at him he smiled and his face became alive. I smiled quickly back then lowered my head out of respect. As he passed by he patted my head gently and I brought my hand up and touched the spot were his fingers had been and stared after him in a dreamlike state. He gave me a little wink and then he was gone from my sight.

Someone roughly shouldered me and knocked me back to reality and I set off home. All the way I could not shake him from my thoughts. I decided I would work twice as hard so that I might be entrusted to go the market again and maybe catch a glimpse of my mythical man.

Disappointingly the days mingled into weeks and the weeks into months and I never saw him again. I was beginning to think I had imagined him. I had my eleventh birthday and we had a small party before the girls started work upstairs. We had settled into a routine and I found that sometimes a whole day would go by and I had not thought of home. I missed them dearly but a child so young adapts to new surrounding and I had adjusted to my new family.

Mother seemed to be adapting too. I didn't really see much of her compared to when we lived on the farm but when we could we cuddled together and she would sing me lullabies and we would play games. I had my daily routine worked out and I carried my chores out perfectly and without complaint but every time I was outside my eyes would dart about looking for the man that haunted my dreams.

Chapter Two

The next three years flew by, mainly because nothing changed. The routine was set and we all followed it, day after day after day. I had seen my fourteenth birthday pass and I was becoming a young woman. My figure had developed and my beautiful curly hair hung down to my waist. The girls had successfully kept me hidden from Augustus. He rarely ventured into the basement and when he did you could hear him and smell him well before you saw him. I had come to realise that my mother was not a housekeeper. I had crept on a few occasions to the basement door and I could always here lots of men cheering. I knew it was something bad but in my innocence I could not work out what it was.

I now went to market twice a week and I knew the stallholders by name. I never revealed where I was from for fear of Augustus rediscovering me. Everyone was nice and I even ran the odd errand here and there for a few coins. I always bought my mother something a little special either a cake or some fresh fruit. She worked such long hours and never had a day off. I had such an easy time of it compared to her.

Each time I went for our food supplied my eyes would scan the crowds meticulously for that stranger I had seen all those years ago. My juvenile eyes that had first seen him had turned him into an unattainable dreamlike figure. I remembered every detail of our brief encounter and I could recall it at will.

On that particular day I had returned from the market and handed the food over to one of the newer girls, Dalphina, who regularly cooked, she was a slightly heavy set girl in her early twenties and had only been with us a year. She was very shy but because were quite close in ages we became good friends.

"They are drawing the baths a bit later tonight if you'd like one?" She asked taking the basket from me.

"Oooh yes please." I answered.

We only got to bathe once a week and it was usually during the day and by the time it was my turn the water was dirty and cold but I would force myself in and scrub down quickly. If they were drawing the baths later on the other girls would have to be quick and I had the chance of getting tepid to warm bath water.

The girls bathed and dressed for work upstairs and I was left all by myself. I tested the water in our three large tubs and was surprised to find one was really warm. I smiled, unfastened my stolla and stepped in the water.

It was wonderful. I sat down with the water coming up to my chin and used a rough bar of soap to wash my skin and hair. I lay there till my skin went wrinkly then I stood up, grabbed a threadbare cloth and began to dry myself. The air was warm and a slight breeze blew through the doorway and I watched in fascination as my breasts and nipples tightened and goose bumps travelled over my body. I went over to our counter that held hairpins and oils for our skin and hair and I began gathering up my tresses.

"Who the hell are you!" The voice boomed into the room and I whirled round, still naked to see Augustus in the doorway. He looked older and much fatter than I remembered from our one and only brief encounter. I screamed and grabbed my stolla from the floor and desperately tried to shield myself.

"I said, who the hell are you?" He repeated just as loud.

"Ginetta." I stammered

"Ginetta?" He looked at me as if trying to remember.

"Yes sir, I am Vianne's daughter, sir. You put me to work down here sir."

"Vianne's daughter." He looked puzzled "Good lord Vianne's been here years. I'll see her whipped for keeping you down here."

"No sir, please don't hurt her."

"Oh, you'll be put to work my little pretty one. By keeping you hidden she might have even done me a huge favour." He suddenly smiled and it was a smile like an asp in your bed before it bites you.

He left me to dress and returned upstairs. I refastened my clothes as fast as I could and heard people coming down the basement steps.

"Why was he down here?" My mother sounded inconsolable.

"I have no idea, it's very suspicious he never leaves the bar unattended even if I'm there." Drusilla answered.

"Oh god he's going to put her to work. Did he touch you sweetie?"

"No momma."

"Still why did he come down here?" Drusilla asked herself.

"I know." Both women turn to see another one of the worker slaves who had followed them. Sihara was an exotic beauty with skin the colour of baked bread.

"Well!" My mother said impatiently

"It was Dalphine. I heard her tell Augustus that there was something stashed in the bathroom he might want to see."

"Dalphine, the little traitor. Sihara is she with a client?"

"No ma'am, it's her time so she is serving drinks."

"Take over and send her down here immediately"

I had never seen Drusilla look so mad. Her cheeks were flushed and she gritted her jaw, curling her lip.

"I thought Dalphine was my friend." I said shyly

"Oh that one has had us fooled."

Drusilla motioned for us to follow her and we padded through to our kitchen and sat at one of the benches. My mother drummed her fingers impatiently on the rough wood and I sat timidly next to her. I wanted ask what work I was going to be made to do and was so bad but in all honesty I was petrified. When Dalphine entered the room she looked surprised and completely innocent.

"What is it Drusilla?" She said sweetly and I almost believed it was impossible that she would have shopped me to horrible Augustus.

"You know what this is about. You told Augustus about Ginetta."

"I wouldn't!" She replied looking shocked.

"Oh really. Vianne go and fetch Augustus, if you are lying believe me your punishment will be ten times worse." Drusilla's words were as cold as ice and I saw Dalphine's face drop. Augustus owned the villa and all the women who lived within its walls but Drusilla managed those women and the villa, everyone knew that she had nearly as much power. My mother got up to leave.

"Ok I did it!" She said suddenly "As soon as I did I regretted it though"

"You stupid little bitch." My mother shouted and in one motion slapped Dalphine hard in the face knocking her to the floor. "Do you know what you have done. Another year or two and we could have snuck her out of here. She could have had a normal life and now she is condemned to service tired old Romans until she is either too old or dies from disease."

"I was normal." Dalphine shouted. "I was betrothed to our governor's son and now look at me. Why the hell should she get to go and live a normal life while I'm forced to do the most horrible things."

"It is done now." Drusilla said calming herself. "Vianne you have to prepare her or it will be a big shock."

My mother nodded tears welling up in her eyes. "

As for you little Dalphine," Drusilla said sinisterly, "I will make sure that for the next month you service the lowest, smelliest and most obscene men that frequent this villa. Your price will be lowered accordingly"

"Drusilla no, please."

"It's too late for please. Maybe then you will learn about loyalty. Now go."

"You take the night off Vianne and I will cover for you. Explain everything. I know it will be hard for you but you must for her own sake."

My mother nodded and waited until we were alone before she spoke.

"You're scaring me momma."

"Oh honey you have no idea and I have no idea how to begin telling you."

"Just tell me."

"Do you know what we do upstairs Gina?"

"No momma, I sorta worked out it isn't nice"

"No it isn't, it's disgusting and degrading and insulting. If your father could see us now…" She stopped, bit her lip for a few seconds and turned her face away. "He would be ashamed. I would rather him think I was dead. My one redemption, my one consolation was that you had been spared. By some miracle you had escaped it or so I thought. This is a house of ill repute Gina. The worst kind. It's a cheap brothel were the dregs of Rome seek their pleasure and we are the receptacles of it."

"Momma?"

"You know about making babies do you not."

"Yes, but I thought only you and Da.."

"No, well in an ideal world yes, but I'm not a wife now Ginetta I'm a slave. A prostitute and I've done things that would make your hair fall out."

I began to cry and my mother wrapped her arms protectively around me.

"Oh honey and by protecting you I have handed Augustus a money making deal I'm sure."

"What do you mean?"

"You're innocence my love. You are a stunning beauty Gina and a virgin. I'm sure Augustus is thinking of ways he can benefit most from it."

"What will we do? We could run away."

"Run away where? How far do you think a woman and a child would get before one of the slave catchers found us?"

"So we just put up with it?"

"Gina this isn't some fairy tale where someone will come along and rescue us this is reality. All I can do is prepare you, and Drusilla will make sure that you don't get any of the stranger clients. If need be I will cater to those."

When dawn approached and the girls came back downstairs to wash I was still awake. My mother had heated some stew but I felt so sick that it lay by my bed untouched.

Drusilla came into see me. She sat softly by my head and stroked my hair. I looked up to her face.

"It won't be so bad. We will all help you ok."

I tried to smile and nod. She kissed the top of my head much like my mother often did and closed my eyes wishing I would wake up and be back on our farm.

The next night I was dressed in a much fancier stolla and went upstairs with the rest of the girls. Augustus pulled me aside.

"Ravishing, simply ravishing. You will be working tables for a few weeks, I've set up an auction for your innocence my dear, and there's already a bidding war, it's splendid!" He clapped his hands together and laughed heartily.

"Take this jug of wine, move from table to table. If anyone enquires about you direct them to me, ok?"

I nodded.

"You carry on looking just like that, absolutely petrified," he chuckled, "it makes your innocence far more appealing."

He turned and left me. Drusilla approached.

"Ok little one, I'm going to tell you how it all works up here ok?"

"Yes Drusilla."

"Now we currently have twenty seven women slaves working here and we all work every night. Have you had your womanly time Gina?"

I nodded; I had got my first period some three months earlier.

"Right, well, when it is a woman's time, she tends the bar and strips the beds and such."

She led me through the bar to a corridor with doors either side. She opened one to reveal a simple bed.

"This is where we entertain. The girls who are working mingle with the guests, laughing and joking and if they want to hire us then we go to one of these rooms to service them. Some of us have higher prices than others. I'm the most expensive so I maybe only have one or two clients each night, your mother is next, so it's not as bad for her as once it was. We are good at what we do and clients will pay for that. Once you finish with a client you wash and head back out. A non working girl will be on stand-by with fresh water, soap and a change of clothes.

Now in a sense you have a little advantage, usually when Augustus brings me a new slave she is given a couple of hours to rest and is then put to work. We have a lot of clients that will pay to be the first to break in a new slave."

She looked at my shocked face.

"Ginetta my child, you have to get used to this world, it's your world too now."

I served drinks for the first time that night and I did it to the best of my ability it wasn't in my nature to be any other way. I had a really silly notion that if I an excellent bartender then perhaps I could do that instead of... well, *you know.* The men who attended Augustus's brothel were as Drusilla had described, mostly dirty and smelly lower class citizens. I was happy to see that my mother seemed to have the pick of whom she could sit with and she was chatting merrily to some young soldiers. I felt slightly guilty as Dalphine had seemingly been put on some sort of special offer and I think I counted her being led into the back room on half a dozen occasions. Augustus tended the busy bar, happy in his kingdom, as sleazy as it was. My feet grew heavy as I was not used to working at night and by dawn I thought I might sleep where I stood.

As mother led me downstairs I heard Augustus telling Drusilla how pleased he was with my behaviour and to see to it that I kept it up. Mother and I went straight to our beds where she hugged me close and I allowed the tears to flow freely. My mother reassured me that it wouldn't be so bad. She would make sure I was shielded from the worse. It didn't reassure me at all. At any given moment my innocence could be stripped from me. I had always dreamed I would lose my virginity to the one I loved; now I prayed to god it was just someone normal.

It was the same for the next four days. It was mother's time, so we worked side by side which was a small blessing. We stripped the beds together and I forgot briefly my horrible fate. I tried to be as grown up and realistic as I could. We couldn't run away. There was a small army of men called slave hunters you could hire for a relatively small fee to round up runaways and they were good at their jobs. In fact they took great delight in recapturing slaves and we heard horrible stories of what happened to the women slaves in particular when they were caught. I looked at my mother in a new light. I thought of everything she had endured over the years so that I could remain safe and now I had to do the same. I had to be brave and show her I was no longer a child, I was a young woman.

I set about my tasks with gusto, if I had to do this type of degrading work I was determined to do it well so that I might only have one or two clients like Drusilla and my mother.

One morning after work I felt famished and I ate a whole bowl full of broth and some bread. My mother smiled to see me finally eat something and then we cuddled up on our bed together. There wrapped in her arms I could be ten-year-old Ginetta. I asked her to sing to me and she smiled then sang a lullaby softly.

Sleep baby sleep,
Shy your eyes and sleep
Have no worries or troubles my dear
Sleep baby sleep

I felt my eyes grow heavy and I drifted off safe in my mamma's arms.

We were awoken what felt like a short time later by Augustus barging in.

"Gather her things she is being moved today. Oh and dress her in one of the finer Stollas."

My mother panicked.

"Where are you taking her?"

"No one was more surprised than I when Maricius paid me a visit I can tell you and he made me an offer that I simply could not turn down."

"Maricius, you mean she is going to the…."

"The Gilded Swan, aye."

"No please Augustus I will work twice as hard I swear just keep her here."

"My dear you would have to work ten clients a night for next three years to earn what I got for the little one. Now no more arguing I'm delivering her in an hour."

He grunted and left the room my mother turned to me.

"I did not foresee this." Her brow creased with worry.

"Where am I going?"

"To the Gilded Swan, another brothel across town."

"No mamma, please I can't do this without you."

"We have no choice. They will treat you a lot better there, honey. I just wish I could join you."

"Why can't you?" I said

"I am too old to work there, they only pick the most stunning beauties."

"You are beautiful mamma."

"Yes but at thirty I am past it to any brothel but this type." I started to cry and she hugged me close, "Now we will still get to see each other. I can go to market and I have spoken to Maricius's wife, Colette on several occasions and she is firm but fair."

"Oh mamma," I sobbed. I had just accepted my fate now I had been dealt another terrible hand to deal with.

I didn't own much, all my belongings fitted in a small cloth bag. I was dressed, as instructed in a lovely Stolla of cream with a thin gold trim. I left my mother and headed bravely upstairs, I heard her sob as I opened the basement door and yet I couldn't go back and comfort her, Augustus was waiting and when he saw me hesitate he grabbed my wrist and led me out of the villa and into the street.

"I don't want any trouble." He barked as he led me along. "The deal is done and dusted, you cause a scene and I'll see to it your mother gets punished, got it."

"Yes sir, I won't cause any trouble."

We stopped outside a huge town Villa. The front door was open and people were milling in and out. Augustus led me inside and up to the bar. I looked around. The room was huge. Several marble tables were set neatly around the room and sat at them were families and couple eating from delicious smelling food. I could tell by the way they were dressed that these were the richest of Rome's citizens. Several girls were serving wine and bringing food out. They were all stunning, dressed in fine material and jewellery, smiling politely.

"This is the girl Colette." Augustus told a heavyset woman behind the bar.

"Good good, I will take her through the back."

"Is Maricius not here?"

"A little too much wine and folly, he is nursing a sore head."

"Such is life." He chuckled,

"Indeed, well I can't chat, I have a busy day so I'll bid you goodbye."

"Of course, well thank you, good day."

I was relieved to be out of Augustus's sight but equally afraid of this woman who seemed so intimidating.

"Salina," she yelled through a door to rear of the bar, "attendance please."

A small woman in her early twenties appeared and took Colette's place.

"Come child I'll show you to your room."

I followed quietly behind as she led me through the back. We entered a large kitchen where several older women were cooking, cleaning dishes and scrubbing pots. I was taken through another door, which opened into a corridor. It was extremely long and at the far end was a right turn.

"This part of the villa is where the slaves all live. There is a central courtyard were you can take small walks to get fresh air. Your room is the first one here. It is our smallest but we are filled to capacity at the moment."

She opened the door. What was small to her certainly wasn't to me. I had slept in a small bed with my mother for the last four years. The room was plain but clean with white plaster walls, a simple bed and a large storage trunk. The floor was made of stone with a small reed mat by the bed.

"It's lovely, thank you." I said not wanting to be impolite.

"I don't have much time to explain the way things work, but I take you know why you are here?"

"Yes mam."

"Good, that's one surprise I don't want to deal with again."

"Now we do things very differently here from any other similar establishment in Rome. During the day we are an expensive eatery where we feed the wealthiest citizens of Rome and their families. At night those same men come back and are serviced by the most beautiful woman that we have to offer. We have thirty-two girls now that you have joined us and they work a rota so that there are always around twenty working at night. We allow the girls one day off a month to do as they please once it has been established that they can be trusted. If you aren't working the floor at night and it isn't your day off then you work the tables during the day."

I was trying my best to fight back the tears but I was so overwhelmed.

"Come now child, this isn't simply a brothel. Our girls are schooled in dance and music to entertain our guests. After ten years we offer our slaves the chance to buy their freedom."

My head shot up at this and she laughed.

"I thought you might like that and you are young. Our clients pay annually for their membership and that is more than enough to satisfy my greedy little husband. Our girls often receive tips or jewellery if they become a favourite, and we allow the girls to keep any gifts they are given. Now I'm pretty sure that Augustus would have worked you to the bone for the ten years if he lives that long. You will find our pace here is more laid back, more sensual. Now you will be given time to adapt, it usually takes around two months to train a girl."

"Train?" I asked warily.

"The first month you will spend several hours a day learning an instrument and being taught to dance. The second month one of our more experienced girls will help prepare you to please our clients. Now I must take my leave. The only thing you need worry about is my bloody husband. As long as I'm here you need not worry. If we do get a virgin I like to offer her to our more prominent clients, my husband always has other ideas. Just try to stay out of his way

"Yes mam"

"Now the day is almost finished, no point in me putting you out to work tables. Unpack your belongings, rest and tomorrow at dawn you start you new working day"

"Yes mam."

"Good."

She spun on her heals and shut my door behind her. I missed my mother terribly already. I wondered if I would be better off at her side or at this new grand place I had been sold to. If Colette was being honest and would get the opportunity to keep any money I was given then there were possibilities. If I saved enough I could buy my mother's freedom. I could buy my own freedom and then we would be free.

It took just two minutes to unpack my belongings. A broach and some simple stollas now sat in the bottom of the large trunk.

I rested a little on my bed and found it to be far comfier than I was used to. I then decided to go for a small walk in the courtyard Colette had mentioned. I walked to the end of the corridor and followed it round. There were gates half way along that took me to the garden and the corridor bent round again so the garden/courtyard was hidden within, only accessible by that one gate. The garden was extremely well kept with orange and lemon trees. There were several benches in the centre and I saw a dark haired girl sat at one of them. I approached her. Like all the other young girls I had seen she was beautiful. Her hair was almost black and she had it tied into a messy bun. She looked up and smiled.

"Hello, you must be the new girl?" Her voice rang with confidence and her hazel eyes smiled with friendship.

"Yes, I'm Ginetta."

"I'm Anazia."

"Are you a slave?"

"Well not as such. My family has fallen on hard times and my daddy sold me into service for two years."

"Good lord." I said shocked

"Aw it's not that bad. This place is famous you know. Everyone in the Roman Empire is gossiping about it. When my father told me I was to work here I was so excited."

"Excited." I answered in disbelief

"Yes, wait till you see the girls Ginetta, I'm so envious. I'm learning dance at the moment and next week I'll be taught by the other girls how to please a man, I already know a thing or two though." She chuckled. I was even more shocked, she didn't look much older than me.

"How old are you." I asked her

"Fifteen."

"And you are not bothered that you will be a... a prostitute." I whispered the last word.

"Oh Ginetta, these girls are far too upper class to call themselves that. And the men, *phew*. We'll sneak along tonight and you'll see."

I wasn't sure if I wanted to but I knew I had to prepare myself. I felt wariness and slight relief at Anazia's enthusiasm.

"Have you met Maricius yet?"

"No, I only arrived a short time ago."

"He is a card let me tell you."

"What do you mean?"

"Well my father agreed to put me into service and Maricius was under the impression that I was a virgin."

She heard my gasp.

"I know! I was nervous as hell that I was going to be found out and then slimy Maricius comes along telling me he's going to break me in half at the first opportunity and I was so scared I was going be found out."

"What happened?" I said with anticipation

"He visited my bed chamber last week."

"And."

"He is under the impression that he took my innocence. He was so blind drunk and his member was so damn small I think he might have mistaken my grandmother for a virgin."

"Anazia!"

"I was so relived."

"How can you be so relaxed about it?"

"I used to love a tumble with the local boys back home. It's natural, there's no need to be ashamed Ginetta. Sex is a beautiful, pleasurable thing. You'll see."

"I just can't imagine it."

"I have to get back to the kitchen but I'll come get you and together we will see what the Gilded Swan has to offer OK?"

She jumped up and practically skipped out of the corridor leaving me even more confused. I had no idea that young girls had sex outside of marriage by choice. I felt so naive. Anazia obviously relished the thought of being a lady of the night but I could not see myself in that role.

My mind drifted to my mystery man. He was the only one I could ever imagine being with and I always fantasised myself in a wifely role. Was it too much to ask that I be a wife rather than a prostitute? Had I somehow angered the gods so much that this was my destiny or had I somehow pleased them that they moved me to the Gilded Swan and away from the claws of the great sweaty Augustus.

Chapter Three

I returned to my room lost in my thoughts and fears. Several hours passed and I watched the sky darken from the tiny window in my bedroom. The corridor outside became busier and busier as the girls woke and prepared themselves for work. There appeared to be much merriment and I could hear the girls laughing and joking with each other. The corridor soon grew quiet once more and shortly after there was a soft rapping at my door and Anazia popped her head around

"Come on." She whispered.

"I'm not sure." I replied with hesitation

"Oh come on, the sooner you see the better."

She was right, the sooner I saw my fate the easier it would be. We tiptoed through to the kitchen and opened the door to the main hall a fraction. From this angle I couldn't see over the top of the bar but Anazia instructed me to stand on a nearby table and look again. I gasped in shock and I was quickly shushed.

There were around twenty girls in the room and they were all naked. Their bodies were free of hair and draped with fine jewels. Some had delicate chains around their waists; others had masses of gold draped round their necks.

Some of them were pale skinned and I saw one woman with skin so dark and majestic it took my breath away. Their skin had been oiled and shimmered under the dull lights of the oil lamps. After my initial shock I could not help but be in awe of them. They looked like goddesses. They flitted about the guests, talking merrily. All the men I saw looked very distinguished and used to the parade of naked young women. I saw nothing of the type we used to get at Augustus's place, these men were handsome and had an air of aristocracy. Soon the women settled with one man or with a group of men, laughing, joking and it all seemed so genuine. On the bench nearest to me sat two young Roman men and a blond girl. I couldn't tell her age but her long mane of hair was peppered with small silver roses. The man sat to her right whispered something in her ear and she looked down and smiled. Her head bobbed down and the man rolled his head back in bliss. I craned my neck to see what was going on but the bar obscured my view. The man sat to her left stood up and rearranged the girl so she was on all fours on the table I could see her clearly now. The first man stood at her head and I saw in horror that he was clutching his manhood firmly, which he offered to the girl. She took it without hesitation and he began pumping in and out of her mouth. She laved it, savoured and the man seemed to enjoy this very much. He lost both his hands in her hair, the strands from her face and he watched as she worked. The second man approached the girl from behind and reached in between her legs. She wiggled her bottom encouraging him. He placed a gentle firm slap on one of her bum cheeks and teased the flesh. After a minute or so he lifted the front of his toga, lifted one leg on to the table and had entered the girl from behind. I was horrified and yet I could not look away. As I glanced around the room I saw that similar things where going on everywhere. On one table two girls were kissing and playing with each other's breasts while half a dozen men watched on. I watched in utter amazement as one girl bent down on all fours, giving the men behind her a view that made their spectators elbow each other and cheer. She then began to feast upon the other girl who wantonly parted herself with her fingers. I stepped down and Anazia climbed up to get a peek.

"Aren't they magnificent?" She whispered. "Woo hoo, look at Phelina, one at the front and one up the rear, lucky cow!"

It suddenly dawned on me that I would have to do those. Not just please one man but maybe two or even a whole group.

I felt bile rising in my throat and I ran to a nearby sink and threw up.

"Ginetta," she jumped down and held my hair as I coughed and spluttered. "You are such a baby. Don't you think they are magical looking?"

"Good gods I did not know then men and women did such things."

"Really, how can a girl of your age know nothing?"

I proceeded to tell her all about how my mother, Drusilla and the other girls had kept her a secret in the basement for four years.

"You mean to tell me that you have never even kissed a boy?"

"No, never."

"Gods Gina, no wonder you threw up, if I'd have known I would have told you first, sorry. Look, you got to come round to this idea and quickly. It's almost an honour to work here and it could really help you."

"How?"

"All the eligible men frequent the Gilded Swan, even if they aren't looking for a wife, some look for mistress's. You will not believe how many Senators wives have served time here. A man knows he is getting a wife skilled in pleasure when he picks one who has severed under Colette and Maricius."

"I can't do it Anazia, I can't do those things." I wailed and she gave me a friendly hug, holding me close.

"I'll help you." She soothed. "I'll tell you everything I know and then when your training starts it will not be a shock."

I nodded through my tears.

"Did you see our bathroom?"

I shook my head.

"Come on. Another perk is we can have a hot bath until sunrise."

"Really?"

"Yes, it's kept warm and refreshed regularly for the girls who are working but it's early so we can have a quick dip."

She took my hand and led me to a door that opened up at the far end of the corridor around the courtyard. The door opened into a huge bathroom with two enormous square sunken baths that could easily seat eight people around them.

"Wow!" I gasped

"I know, fancy living huh?" Anazia replied. "They are heated from the basement underneath."

"Really."

"Yes, test it."

I removed my sandal and dipped my toe into the nearest bath. To my surprise it was as if someone had just poured it and the aroma of orange blossom, cherries and lemon filled the air. I turned round and was startled to see that Anazia was totally naked having shed her stolla.

"Come on we haven't got long."

She stepped past me into the bath and sat on the step.

"Hmm I love it when they scent the water, you can smell it on your skin for days. Ginetta come on I won't bloody bite." She laughed

I carefully unclasped the broach holding my stolla together and let it fall to the ground. I kicked off my other sandal and went to get in the other bath.

"Get in this one silly its huge and we can talk, oh and grab one of those pots from the window."

I did as she asked and got in the tub. The water was red hot and the tiles under my feet were almost too hot to even walk on. I handed the tub to Anazia and she opened it and removed a large lump of what looked like purple fat to me.

"It's a special mixture of olive oil, lavender and coarse salt it leaves your skin feeling fabulous. Here try some."

I scooped a little onto my fingertips and began to work the mixture into my arms. The lavender smelt lovely and she was right as I rinsed my skin felt silky smooth. I took some more and began on my legs mirroring exactly what Anazia was doing. I looked at her closely. She really was beautiful, almost gypsy like with her dark features. She had the hugest brown eyes and an oval face with full pouting lips.

"You know I'd never had a bath as hot as this before I came here so I like to come in everyday. When I have to go home to the farm I will miss it." She said almost sadly.

"Is there a special boy at home?" I asked boldly

"Yes." She said longingly.

"Tell me about him?"

"His name is Vitto, the son of the neighbouring farmer and he is twenty years old although I first liked him when I was twelve and he was seventeen"

"Twelve!"

"That's not usual, one of my sisters married at twelve. I was besotted with him but he never looked my way, I was just a child to him. He's the best looking man in our village and I wanted him. I hatched a plan, bided my time, watching him with other girls. When I was fourteen he found me in one of their barns. I had gone there knowing he would be brushing the horses but I claimed to have lost one of our lambs and thought I'd heard it in the barn. I remember him looking at me as if I'd turned into a woman overnight and I wanted him so badly but I acted all innocent. He did the chasing after that, calling round to our farm with eggs and extra milk. If he caught me on the way home he would ask if he could take me into the city for dinner. I refused and refused until I thought I might die from longing for him. I had fumbled around with a couple of local boys before that, nothing heavy, but eventually I gave Vitto my innocence and it was fabulous, Ginetta. You have no idea of the pleasure your body can feel. It's like a flower blossoming into fire. He was heartbroken when I told him I was coming here, but I will be able to visit him on my days off and I get three a month."

"Will you marry him?"

"I don't know, I mean I do love him but I do not know what opportunities might arise from working here. Love is not everything."

We soaked for a little and the water stayed wonderfully hot. When we stepped out Anazia handed us some lovely clean towels from a cupboard at the side and I dried myself liberally then redressed.

"I promise you. You will be fine." She told me again.

I was beginning to think that maybe she was right but I could not bear to think about what would be required of me.

If I was destined to prostitute no matter how much I hated the idea it was surely better to be in the most elaborate one in Rome than the peeling walls of Augustus's house of ill repute.

Anazia saw me back to my bedroom and gave me a friendly hug. I did manage to sleep and I dreamt once more of my mystery man. After what I had seen in the main hall my mind cast him in a different more intimate role. In my dream he approached me from behind running his hands over my body. We kissed passionately and in my dreams he made love to me awakening my body as Anazia had described.

The next morning the sun wasn't even set fully in the sky before Colette banged on my door barking for me to get up to eat breakfast. I got up and dressed in a fresh stolla and made my way to the kitchen. Colette, Anazia and five other girls were there. The chef, an older woman removed a fresh loaf from the oven and the smell made my stomach growl.

"Ok girls," she nodded towards a side table where bread, cheese and fruit were laid out. I followed Anazia's lead and took a plate from a cupboard and loaded it up. This was very elaborate compared to the breakfast I was used to, which was usually day old bread and nothing else. I tried not to look too surprised. We made our way through to the main hall where a single table had been set out. There were two jugs: one containing water, and the other milk. I poured myself some milk and ate my bread, cheese and grapes. The cheese was soft and delicious and the milk was chilled. I thoroughly enjoyed it. We had barely finished when the chef came out and we were shooed back into the kitchen.

"Ok girls you know the drill lets get those tables set out." Her voice boomed out. We set fresh fruit out in platters on the centre of each table as well as more cheese and some slices of salted meat too. Colette kept a watchful eye on us and I dared not speak to any of the other girls I just mimicked exactly as they were doing.

When couples and families started to arrive, Colette was friendly and warm and helped them to their seats. Once there, we had to ask what they would like to drink and clear their plates as they finished eating. It was a well-oiled machine and I had to appreciate how skilled Colette was at running it. If she saw a girl slacking or dawdling in the kitchen they felt the back of her hand on their head but she also praised Anazia for doing really well. It was approaching teatime and our patronage had died down a little.

"Anazia, Ginetta you may have a short break to eat dinner."

We grabbed some bread and salted pork then headed out to the little courtyard.

"The waiting on is so boring."

"I don't mind." I said honestly. I would certainly rather do that than service the men of Rome.

"I cannot wait for my debut night."

"Anazia I don't understand how you can just except this. I mean what kind of father sells his own daughter like that?"

"He's a good man," she said defensively, "we just fell on some hard times. We lost half our cattle last year because of disease. I have nine brothers and sisters."

"Gosh"

"I didn't discourage it, when he suggested it. If I had he would not have forced me."

"How can you give yourself so freely and willingly?"

"Once you realize the power those women have you will embrace it too. Some women, ordinary women, the gods sent to bare children. Women like you and me are destined for greater things. You are beautiful Ginetta and you will hypnotise those men, bend them to your will."

"I didn't see any of that."

"The girl you saw, with the two men."

"Yes?"

"Do you know what arrived for her this morning?"

"What?"

"A solid gold broach inlaid with diamonds and rubies."

"Wow."

"Those men were so captivated by her that one of them sent a beautiful gift. Think what such a treasure could do for you. It could buy your mothers freedom I'll wager."

She saw my eyes widen.

"Yes, so think of the possibilities."

I was. It was churning round in my head over and over. If only I could just accept it. If only I could swallow my pride and be as wanton as Anazia seemed to enjoy being.

"Come on, we best get back. Colette does not like us to be idle."

"I noticed"

The next two weeks were easy. I waited the tables and for two hours a day a retired dancer taught me basic dance moves that I picked up easily. My studies in seduction had begun and I was picking up everything quicker than everyone thought. Anazia was my first real friend and once the girls had started work at night we went to the kitchen, which was large and well lit, and to the music of the great hall we would practice some more. The moves involved long silk scarves. One was secured on each wrist and then to the music you had to dance and the scarves would dance through the air with you. Anazia could do it perfectly, moving her hips and arms in a way that made me envious of her confidence. She was patient with me though and coached me for hours.

I had even got used to Colette and had received several compliments from her. I had managed to avoid the owner Maricius entirely and I was beginning to relax a little. Colette surprised me one evening by asking me to do a small errand for her.

"We have a wine order that was due in today and it's late. I need you to run across town and see why it is late. I do not think we have enough for tonight if they do not deliver it."

"Yes ma'am"

"Straight there and straight back missy."

"Yes ma'am"

"You can stop by the baker at the end of the street and pick me up some sugared plum bread."

She reached under the counter and brought up a small change purse then handed me some coin.

"A warning."

"ma'am?"

"If you run, we will find you and that will be the end of your career at the Gilded Swan and to pay for the cost of buying you I will tie you to a barrel in the courtyard and let the dregs of Rome have a go at you."

I nodded furiously.

"Just let us trust you. It will make your life much easier."

"Yes ma'am, I won't be any bother for you."

"I didn't think that you would really. Now go hurry."

I ran as fast as I could through the cobbled streets of the city, I was determined to be quick and efficient and show Colette how much she could trust me. I made it to the vineyard on the edge of the city in less than thirty minutes I was sure. The owner told me that the order was being loaded on to a cart and would be delivered in less than two hours. I rested for a few minutes and then I set off once more as fast as my sandals would allow me to run. The sun was setting and the sky was dark by the time I made it to the bakers and they were just about to close. The baker smiled kindly though and sold me the bread that Collette had requested, wrapped in thin paper. I was sure I had done well and I ran down the street back to the Gilded Swan.

Suddenly a gentleman who had been talking to his companions at the side of the street stepped back, I was running far too fast, we collided and I went flying onto the street, dropping the bread and grazing my knee quite badly.

"I am terribly sorry my dear."

I felt his hand gently cup my elbow and lift me. My knee protested at the movement and I hobbled and fell into the gentlemen.

"I'm terribly sorry sir…" I looked up and my voice caught in my throat. It was him. It was my dream man. He looked exactly as he had done the day I saw him in the market when I was ten years old, he had not changed.

"Can you walk child?"

My brain wouldn't answer. I blinked to try to find the words to answer him but my heart was pounding wildly in my chest.

"Child?" His voice was as I imagined it would be and it brought tears to my eyes that I had finally heard it. He mistook my tears and thought me to be in pain. In one motion he scooped me up in his arms as if I weighted nothing at all.

"Where do you live?" He asked as he set off walking.

"The Gilded Swan sir." I found my voice and shakily replied.

"You seem so young, well it's no business of mine but I don't want you to get into trouble I'll accompany you and explain to Colette how you hurt your leg. Were you to work tonight?"

"No sir, I have not yet been trained I've only been there a little while."

"How old are you?"

"I'll be fifteen next month."

"Ye gods, a child. Has Maricius got his hands on you?"

"I have not seen him yet sir."

"I sometimes wonder what the world is coming too, I really do." He said to himself more than me.

Colette was waiting at the door and when she saw my mystery man carrying she frowned.

"I hope you have not been causing any trouble Ginetta." She said sternly.

"On the contrary," my hero answered. "I'm afraid I knocked her over and she could not walk, I did not want her to get into trouble so I thought I would bring her home. I will also compensate you for the bread I caused her to drop."

"Not necessary Vincent." Colette replied. "Would you care for a glass of wine?"

"No, no, I haven't the time. I have some important business but thank you."

He set me down gently and I grimaced and looked at my knee which was now swollen and bleeding.

"I hope you feel better Ginetta, and I am sorry again."

"It's fine sir."

"Inside missy," Colette said to me, "let's get you sorted out."

I now had a name for my prince. Vincent. I repeated the information about the wine order to Colette as I struggled through to the kitchen.

"I shall be having words, they know better than to deliver this late. Well you need to go rest and lift that leg up."

"Yes ma'am."

"You have done well Ginetta, despite your mishap."

"Thank you."

"Rest until tomorrow, go."

I could not get to my little room fast enough. I lay on my bed and rested my leg high up on the windowsill. I was so happy. My stomach was doing somersaults as I remember every contour of his sculpted face and huge well-built frame. Suddenly I wished Vincent were one of the customers of The Gilded Swan. He could have me - mind, body and soul. I would do anything, be anything for him. *Why did I feel such a pull towards him when I had only seen him twice?* I could almost feel him running his hands over my body, touching me, caressing me. His fingers, so graceful, dancing on my body. I let out a small moan as my body responded to my thoughts.

"Well, well, well. This must be my newest recruit."

My eyes shot open to see a short, greying man stood in my doorway. I shot up and winced at the pain.

"I bet you were wondering when you would meet me. My wife is currently very occupied accepting the wine delivery so I thought I would pay you a visit."

I had already worked out that this was Maricius and even though Anazia had tried to tell me not to worry about him I was petrified.

"I am going to enjoy breaking you in little one."

I backed myself against the wall and he laughed.

"MARICIUS!"

He grimaced as he heard Colette bellowing from the kitchen.

"What the hell are you doing?"

He had poked his head out of my doorway.

"I was just checking on the girls knee Colette."

"Maricius, I was not born yesterday. The bar is you're responsibility at night."

"Yes dear."

"NOW!"

He jumped up.

"I'll be seeing you later my little blond princess." He whispered

I was terrified that he would come back to my room but thankfully he didn't. I managed to catch an hour of sleep here and there and when Colette woke me the next morning my leg felt a lot better. I hobbled through to the kitchen and I was put on potato peeling duties. I didn't mind it enabled to let my mind freely drift and imagine Vincent. Our two meetings even though short had had a dramatic impact on my small mind. I had to find out more about him, I just didn't have a clue how.

Just after lunch I heard Colette and Maricius having a huge row in the courtyard. I couldn't make out the words but what ever it was Maricius was not for backing down and by the sound of neither was Colette. Maricius stormed into the kitchen and out into the main hall. Colette appeared right after him but she stopped in front of me.

"I do believe it's your lucky day little Ginetta."

"Ma'am?"

"It seems that one of the richest men in Rome has taken quite a shine to you."

"I don't understand."

"Vincent Magnus my dear."

My heart skipped a beat at the mention of his name.

"He came back last night, its lucky I was here late had it just been Maricius I think he would have turned Vincent down flat. He bartered with us and in the end he paid the equivalent of four times what Maricius originally paid for you."

"What?"

"He is collecting you at sunset."

I could not take it in. My savoir, my prince had returned and truly saved me. I didn't care what was to become of me if he was my owner. I smiled widely.

"Maricius did not want to let you go I can tell you, but Vincent has exchanged a large town house that Maricius has wanted for a couple of years. You can stop peeling the potato child." She laughed

"Sorry" I said smiling

She shook her head and shooed me to my room to pack my belongings and wait for him. I couldn't believe it. In my wildest fantasies I could never have imagined that he would return for me. I had a couple of hours till sunset and I decided to nap seeing as I had not got much sleep the night before. I dreamt of Vincent again, dreamt of him carrying me, whispering that he loved me. He dipped his head down and his lips met mine. I was still afraid at the thought of sex but when I paired it with the image of Vincent I felt excited at discovering all the pleasures awaiting me.

"You are a dark horse Ginetta."

Anazia's voice woke me from sleep.

"Hi." I said.

"Tell me it isn't true."

"What?" I said smiling

"I heard Colette telling some of the girls that Vincent Magnus had bought you!"

"It's true." I replied with a smile.

"I am jealous. He is undoubtedly the most gorgeous man I have ever seen and he is one of the wealthiest men in Rome."

"Does he come here then?"

"Are you kidding? Rumour is he has his own harem of women at his villa outside the city and it looks like you are going to be one of them."

"Wow."

"I can't believe you go out for bread and you manage to charm a man like that."

I couldn't help but smile. Even though I had only known Anazia a short I would miss her terribly. She really had been a help to me, at least she was happy to be part of The Gilded Swan, I was not, and now I didn't need to worry about that at all.

"You seem a lot happier"

"I don't see how I could have coped being here Anazia"

"You would have, but I guess you have to only worry about pleasing one man now."

"I'm sorry I won't see your debut."

"I know, it's next week. I just can't wait it's been weeks since I saw any action."

Inside I was positively glowing at that thought. I could not wait to be intimate with Vincent the thought was making me feel light headed and funny.

Anazia stayed in my room until it was dark and Colette popped her head round the door announcing that my new master had arrived. I jumped off the bed and grabbed my bag, gave Anazia a huge kiss on the cheek and practically skipped behind Colette all the way into the main hall. Maricius was behind the bar and when he saw me his face clouded with disappointment and I had to fight the urge to laugh I was so happy.

Outside a beautiful carriage pulled by four white horses waited for me. The door was opened from the inside and I approached without hesitation.

"Now behave for your new master Ginetta."

"Ye ma'am. "I replied.

I reached the doorway, and sat there in all his glory was Vincent. He held his hand out to help me inside, the door was shut and we were on our way.

I was in a daze for the next few minutes because I could not quite believe I was really sat there with him. I was surely back in my bed and I would waken at any second with the fear of Maricius pawing me.

"You are as quiet as a mouse young Ginetta." He said softly. I closed my eyes and listened to the velvet tones of his voice.

"I'm sorry sir."

"Please call me Vincent."

"Vincent."

"That's better. Now tell me. Did any harm befall you, did anyone touch you before our deal went through."

"No one touched me, no one has ever touched me." I wanted him to know that.

"Good. I am happy that you don't have to worry about pleasing dozens of men."

"No, only you now." I said boldly smiling at him.

"Me, what? No Ginetta!"

I was startled.

"I did not buy you so I could put you through those horrors myself. You are just a child and you deserve a childhood."

"I don't understand, Anazia said you had women at your mansion to…"

"That I do. Is that the life you want, for if it is I will take you right back to Maricius. You should want more Ginetta and I intend to give it to you. A child should be given the chance to blossom."

"What do you require of me?"

"A maid recently left my service and I want you to fill her roll."

My face dropped but I tried to regain my composure.

"As well as these light duties I intend to educate you, teach you to read and write."

My mood picked up slightly at this thought.

"When you have served me for a set amount of time I will set you free little Ginetta and you can enter the world fully prepared."

"But why me?" I asked timidly

"You seemed so innocent in my arms and I did not want you to loose that."

"Thank you." I said genuinely.

We rode to city outskirts and Vincent asked me questions about myself I recounted my tale of being captured as best as I could and then told him of my four years at Augustus's and my mothers mission to keep me from harm.

On the surface I was answering his questions but all the while a plan was already forming in my mind. So Vincent saw me as a child and maybe I was. I wasn't yet fifteen but some women back then were married and even had children of their own by thirteen or fourteen. In my mind I knew I was immature mainly because I had not seen much apart from the market place over the last four years. I remembered Anazia telling me how she won her man's heart. She bided her time and was patient and I would do the same with Vincent. He would find the most compliant maid he had ever had and the most eager student too. When the time was right I planned to have my man, I had my heart set on him.

Chapter Four

Vincent's Villa was huge sitting on large open grounds of immaculate landscaped gardens. It had white marble pillars outside the front door. As we drew up a servant appeared and opened the door for us to exit. I trailed behind Vincent, in through the front door and into a large entry hall. Bits of armour littered the walls, battered shields and not so new looking swords were everywhere. A huge stone fire roared along one wall with thick fur throws on the floor in front of it. My eyes drifted back to the armour and I imagined Vincent encased with them.

"My battle gear, displayed to remind me, and anyone entering my home, of all my victories."

How many battles must he have fought in order to have used all these weapons?

"Come, Ginetta."

I followed him through to some living area with comfy overstuffed cushions on the floor and another roaring fire. We continued through to the back of the house past the kitchen to the servants' quarters and he opened a door to a large bedroom.

"This is to be your new room."

"Just for me? All this?"

"Yes," he laughed. "Now it's very late so why don't you rest and then report to our head maid Marvette in the morning OK?"

"Yes Vincent."

"Now I am to be left undisturbed during the day. My business keeps me up through the night and the day is when I rest. If you should need to ask anything you report to Marvette."

"Yes Vincent."

"Good, now I will let you get settled. The staff has gone home for the day so get some sleep and in the morning head for the kitchen"

"Thank you"

"You are most welcome. Sleep well little one you have nothing to fear now."

He said it with such sincerity that I believed him, I believed I was one hundred percent safe in his care. He shut the door leaving me standing in the middle of that grand bedroom looking at the place he had just been stood with longing. I didn't move for the longest time but eventually when I realised he wasn't coming back I dropped my small cloth bag on the floor and warmed my hands a little on the roaring fire. *My very own fire!*

I boldly slept naked in the hope that he would change his mind and return but I awoke the next morning feeling a mixture of relief to be there and disappointment that he seemed to be the only man in Rome who did not want my innocence.

Still I did not want him to let him down in anyway so I dressed in a tunic from one of the trunks and made my way through to the kitchen. There was a lady with her back to me and she turned when she heard my sandals on the marble floor.

"Well hello there child come in, what's your name?" She was an older woman with grey hair and a kind face.

"Ginetta, mam"

"I'm Marvette but everyone calls me May. Have you made bread before?"

"Oh yes." I smiled

"Good well you can help me with this and then we will have some breakfast."

I helped to grind the flour and then to knead the dough and Marvette was suitably impressed.

"It is nice to have some help around here, some more women's help. Vincent has a lot of body guards and there are two girls that will be here shortly but it's nice to have someone on the premises."

"Do you also live here?"

"No but I stay in a small cottage on the grounds so I am here at the crack of dawn."

"I can't believe that only you and two girls manage this huge house."

"There's only really the girls room to look after."

"Girls?"

Vincent's lady friends." She frowned slightly as she answered me.

"Now I don't mind that he has four women to cater to his every whim, I just don't understand why he had to pick four of the most ill-mannered in Rome."

"May?"

"I'm sure you'll see for yourself soon enough we strip their beds and draw their baths late afternoon. Do not speak to them unless it's necessary they will only upset you."

I was slightly worried now. We ate some raisin bread with cheese and drank some hot herbal tea. After that I helped to sweep the floor in the living areas and wipe all the dust away. When the bread was cooked I helped May start to prepare some roasted mutton for that evening's meal. I had never smelt anything so delicious.

"Is this Vincent's favourite meal?"

"It's more for the girls, I hardly see Vincent unless I am here late."

"Does he sleep all day every day?"

"He will emerge now and again if it is important but he owns several taverns across the city so he manages them in the evening."

The two other maids she had mentioned arrived just before lunch and they set about their routine without giving me much thought. I stuck with Marvette, eager to learn everything, anything that would please Vincent. In the afternoon I followed her to the accommodation at the rear of the house, a marble corridor with five doors along it. We both carried handfuls of fresh clean bedding.

"The first one is Vincent's. You don't need to do anything in there."

The next one Marvette knocked lightly.

"Would you like the bed changing miss?"

"No go away!"

I was a little taken aback but May shrugged it off and continued along, knocking on the third."

"Miss, it's Marvette, can I change your linen miss."

There was thumping and groaning then.

"Come in."

We entered the bedroom and the woman in question had got up and sat in a nearby chair. I had thought that my bedroom was elaborate but this room made it look like a shack. The room was so large it needed supporting with four pillars. In the centre of the room was a bed twice the size of mine. The fire had nearly died out and Marvette indicated with a nod of her head that I should put more wood on it. I did while she stripped the huge bed and began dressing it again.

"Who is the child?"

I looked at her from the corner of my eye. There was no denying she was beautiful even in her sleepy state. She had black hair and bright green eyes and a permanent look of contempt.

"This is Ginetta, miss. She's the new maid."

"You just make sure she follows the rules ok."

"Yes Miss."

"And hurry up I want to get back to sleep. What's for dinner?"

"I'm doing roast mutton and vegetables miss."

"Mmm good, do a cake too will you."

"Yes Miss. Will there be anything else?"

"No."

I couldn't believe how rude she was being to Marvette.

"Is she always like that." I whispered as soon as we were safe outside the room.

"Yes, that's Anastasia. She is always bitter and rude."

"What are the rules?"

"I'll explain later, let's get these beds done first."

The next room we didn't even get an answer so we tried the last one.

"Carlina stays in this one, she's the nicest but don't let that fool you."

I nodded hanging on to her every word.

"Come in." came a reply

Carlina was blond and petit and her room was exactly the same size and layout as Anastasia's. She was still in bed when we entered but she stepped out, gloriously naked and reached for a robe on the floor. She surprised me by going to her fire herself and placing two more logs on.

"Dinner smells good May."

"Thank you, miss"

"Hi there" She said addressing me. "You must be Ginetta, Vincent mentioned last night that he was bringing you home. How are you settling in?"

"Fine thank you Miss." I replied keeping my head down.

"Good, May do you think you could wake me well before dinner I want to visit the city."

"Of course Miss."

"In fact, perhaps Ginetta could run my errand for me. I have some new tunics and togas to pick up and I have some of my favourite sugared fruit ordered. Would you be a dear and take the carriage and collect them for me." She smiled so sweetly that I felt I couldn't refuse.

"Of course I don't mind." I replied

She approached a nearby dresser, opened it and removed a handful of coins. Without counting them she handed them to me.

"There's more than enough there and you can keep the change."

She gave me directions to the two shops that were in the wealthiest part of Rome. I had been so eager to go to the city because I wanted to let my mother know I was ok.

When we had finished in Carlina's room we headed back to the kitchen.

"She could have asked one of the guards to run that errand." May said angrily.

I don't mind." I said defensively.

"I know you don't my dear but she has only done it so you know your place."

"Oh. Perhaps you should tell me these rules"

"Of course, I had forgotten. Apart from to change the beds you are never to go into the back of the house and never under any circumstances do you go into Vincent's room, he values his privacy above everything else."

"That is a small thing to ask in return for everything he has done for me."

"Well you'd better go. Don't worry I'll keep you some mutton warmed."

"We get the mutton too."

"Yes," she laughed. "Now go or it will be midnight before you get back."

May went outside to the stables and told the driver to bring the carriage round while I went to add a large sash over my tunic for warmth. When the carriage came round I gave the instructions to the driver and luckily he was familiar with both places I needed to go.

The drive to the city was lovely and it reminded me a lot of our home. The fields of crops and cattle took me back to those carefree days on the farm with my brothers. It seemed a lifetime ago. I picked up the clothes from the tailor and the sugared fruit from a delicatessen nearer the centre of the city. Then I asked the driver to take me to Augustus's house. I explained it was just a short visit to see my mother but he didn't question me.

Augustus's Villa looked even more rundown and shabby even though it was just only weeks since I had last worked there. I went to the garden round the back. There were windows in the ground at the back of the house with bars on and these were the slaves' bedrooms. I went to the one I knew used to be ours and I removed a coin from my little cloth pouch and I clinked it lightly on the bars. At first no one came so I clinked a little harder. Then Drusilla appeared. Her eyes adjusted to the light and then her face lit up with recognition.

"Ginetta, how are you?"

"I'm fine, where's my mother. I bought her some sugared fruit."

"Wonderful news sweetie. I wouldn't have believed it myself. Last night a very prominent businessman of Rome came in, bought your mother and would you believe it has set her working in one of his shops. It doesn't make sense."

"It was Vincent." I whispered

"How did you know?" She said puzzled

"He is my new owner, he bought me from The Gilded Swan last night to be a maid at his villa and last night in the carriage I told him all about my mum."

"You lucky thing. Your mother didn't know, she said she was going to head for The Gilded Swan as soon as she could. Go see her, the shop is only on the next street, the dry provisions one"

"Thank you Drusilla, Thank you for everything, perhaps we will be able to save you as well."

"I have had ample opportunity to leave here little one. I am waiting for Augustus to pop off. He has no children, thank the gods so I am being left everything."

"I miss you." I said touching her hand through the bars.

"And I you, you are the best of us all."

I reached into my tunic and withdrew my coin pouch once more and emptied out all the change and handed it to Drusilla through the bars. She looked at it.

"What's this for honey?"

"I want you to have it."

She looked at the coins, then back at me, her face full of love.

"Thank you, sweet heart. I am glad it turned out well for you."

I left and told the driver wait where he was for me and I skipped around to the shop. It sold grains and dry ingredients for cooking. I knew it because I had been in on many occasions. I skipped in the door and there behind the counter was my mother.

I ran immediately to her and threw my arms around her.

"Ginetta what are you doing here, do they know you are out?" She looked worried so I explained about Vincent buying me, and him being the one who had also bought her.

"I was so confused Gina, he said he would return this evening to explain everything but he seemed in a frightful rush to get back home. I can't believe he has done this. I even have my own room upstairs and I get a wage. Just like that I am a free woman." Her eyes filled with tears and we hugged again.

"I don't want to stay too long mama but I'm sure I will be able to return often. I was only sent out to run errands I don't want to anger anyone."

"Quite right honey. I intend to be the best worker he has ever had."

"Me too."

Back at the mansion I headed straight for the kitchen and happily recounted my tale to Marvette who served me up some delicious Mutton with vegetables and gravy.

"Vincent is a good man through and through." She said. "I was a slave too. An older slave with no use and Vincent bought me and brought me here. I've served him for around ten years and I will do so until I am physically unable."

I was moved by her dedication to him. It seemed Vincent had touched so many lives.

Shortly before the sun set all the maids left. I had counted five guards pacing the grounds and they remained.

I padded through to the living room and sat in front of the fire.

"Good evening Ginetta."

His deep voice interrupted my thoughts and I turned to see Vincent stood in the doorway. I couldn't help it, I jumped up and ran to him hugging him fiercely, and he was as solid as stone. He seemed startled at first but soon I felt his chest vibrate as he chuckled.

"What has brought this on?" He asked

"My mother, you saved her."

"How did you know?"

"I ran an errand for Carlina and I stopped by to let her know I was OK."

"I was going to surprise you but no matter. I don't want you running errands for my girls, that's not what you are here for. I will tell them."

"I don't want to get anyone in trouble, I didn't mind honestly."

"You are more here to help Marvette, the girls have plenty time on their hands for errands and you will have one day off a week to visit your mother."

"One day a week!" I said in disbelief.

"Yes." He chuckled. "Now child, come on sit down and we will begin your tutoring."

The next few months flew by. My duties as a maid were simple and pleasurable. I got to know Marvette really well. I totally avoided Vincent's four girls, and apart from to change their beds twice a week, I rarely saw them as they kept their hours similar to Vincent's. When they did surface I retreated to my bedroom and kept out of the way.

True to his word Vincent began tutoring me. He taught me to read and write. We also touched on geography and arithmetic too. I wasn't really that keen to learn but it meant spending time with the man I had come to adore.

I waited with anticipation each evening for him to come to the living room for our lessons to begin. Sometimes we sat in his study and while he worked I would sit at the side of his desk and work. Other times if Vincent was lecturing me we strolled in the grounds delighting in the night air. He was as unattainable as ever to me. My heart ached for him and yet I did not want to jeopardize the time we spent together. The timing was not right for me to reveal the extent of my love for him.

I visited my mother every week and she was as happy as I could ever remember her being. I think she was even having a relationship with a local merchant who was a widower. She was putting all her money aside for retirement so that when she was unable to work she could afford to be taken care of.

My fifteenth birthday passed and Vincent bought me a gold broach inlaid with emeralds. I wore it every day and cherished it.

One evening I was feeling a little under the weather and retired to my bed earlier than usual. I was burning a little fever and was restless all night. I heard giggling outside my door in the dead of night. It faded as the person walked out of earshot. I tiptoed out of bed and opened my door. I caught a glimpse of Vincent arm in arm with Carlina rounding the corner into the accommodation wing. I knew I shouldn't, but I followed and they disappeared into Vincent's room. They left the door slightly open almost inviting me to look.

I felt so guilty, if I was caught I would be in big trouble but the prospect of seeing Vincent relieved of his clothes was far too tempting.

I debated what to do for a few more minutes then approached the door and the thin sliver of light escaping from the room through the crack.

They were both naked and stood by the blazing fire. My mind barely registered Carlina's perfect body, my focus was on Vincent. He was glorious and majestic. His shoulders were broad and his chest tapered. It seemed every bit of flawless skin covered solid muscle. My eyes travelled down. The only men I had seen intimately had been that one evening at The Gilded Swan but surely my mind had been playing tricks on me for it seemed Vincent was double that size. His member was standing erect and proud and Carlina was caressing it with one hand whilst he lifted her hair up and planted small kisses on her shoulders and neck. She was already moaning but when his other hand drifted to her breast kneading and teasing her nipple she let out little cries. I was transfixed.

"Are you hungry tonight my love?" She said huskily

"Ravenous." He replied.

"Then feast Vincent, have your fill and fill me."

He laughed softly and guided her backwards towards the bed. I shifted myself slightly so I could still see them. Vincent had laid her softly on the bed and seemed to enjoy caressing her skin. She in return moaned and purred like a cat in heat. He positioned himself between her legs and I could see the look of pure lust on Carlina's face. The muscles in his back were perfectly defined and his buttocks were tight and bronzed, the slightest movement saw them flex and twitch.

"Hmm you definitely are a feast my little Carlina."

"Stop talking Vincent honey."

He laughed again as she hooked one of her feet round his back and urged him forward. He guided himself into her and she threw her back in ecstasy. I could not take my eyes off her expression. She had arched her back so all weight was on her shoulders and bottom. Her cries got louder and louder until I thought about leaving scared someone else might come out to see what the noise was about.

"Now Vincent!"

I looked up at him and I gasped. I could only see part of his face but there was no denying that two of his teeth had become long sharp fangs. He smiled and in one motion he dipped his head and bit her neck.

She did not protest, the opposite in fact. Her screams grew louder and louder still and I could see blood gathering on the sheets below where his face was still buried in her neck. He was now pumping in and out of her at an impossible speed until he withdrew from her neck and let out a loud moan and began to slow his pace.

"Mmm you were hungry."

"And you were loud."

"I like to remind the other girls who your favourite is."

"I think they know." He answered with a chuckle.

"Can I stay with you?"

"Yes for a time but return to your own room at dawn"

I ran back to my own room and contemplated what I seen. To this day I do not know why I did not flee. I associated fangs with evil and even though I knew I was in love with Vincent I should have had the sense to leave. Yet I was not scared. In fact I imagined being in Carlina's place. I imagined Vincent biting me, making love to me and I could not get that image out of my head.

I did not understand what he was and I was so confused, wound up and deeply jealous that for the next few days I was not myself. I pieced together Vincent's oddities, I had never seen him eat and I rarely saw him in the daylight hours and I had definitely never seen him step outside the Villa in the day. He knew so much, about the past, about different cultures and religions. I knew this must all lead back to what he was. Baffled though I was, I knew one thing for certain. I would never betray him. My discovery had also given me an advantage. When the timing was right I knew how to tempt him, I knew what he craved.

Chapter Five

I do not want to go over the next couple of years in detail. It was some two thousand years ago and a lot of it I can't remember. I never tried to spy on Vincent again I would have loved to see him again in all his naked glory but the thought of him with other girls was not one I relished. I sat on the sidelines ever the spectator and the keeper of his dark secret. I knew Vincent had grown fond of me. My studies had long since stopped yet he would sit and debate or talk things over with me. I fitted well into his busy life. I was always keen to listen to him talk whatever the subject. I only half listened to the words he spoke I was hypnotised by the drawl of his voice. As my mind matured my love for him grew. I silently adored him, worshiped him. I cleaned and kept his house better than any other maid and I did it because I so wanted to please him. As I blossomed into a woman I hoped he might see me in a new light. I wanted to see lust in his eyes. It was never ending torment that I endured out of love.

I was eighteen then, no longer a child. It was frustrating that eyes would follow me when I visited the town yet Vincent, the only man I ever wanted, could not look upon me that way. He still saw me as a fourteen-year-old girl. One evening Vincent surprised me by coming to the living room while the sun was not quite set.

"Gina?" He said using the little nickname he called me, which I adored. "Can you come to the study?"

I thought nothing of it and followed behind him. However once he sat down I saw his face was unusually serious.

"Vinnie, what's the matter? Have I done something?"

"Not at all but I have come to a decision and it saddens me a little."

"What is it?"

"When I bought you Gina I told you I wanted you to be in my service for a set amount of time. I am ashamed to admit that that time is long up. I had planned to set you free on your seventeenth birthday but Marvette adores you and I have grown fond of you being around."

"I don't want to leave here." I said panicking

"Gina, come now, there is a life waiting for you outside of this Villa. I have put aside a wage for you every week. He reached under his toga and removed a large coin purse brimming with money."

"Keep it, let me stay, don't send me away. This is my home."

"It would be selfish to keep you Gina, my mind is made up. At the end of this week you are free little one."

I started to sob and he came round to comfort me.

"You could do anything Gina. Marry, have children, be happy. You could even buy a little shop for you and your mother. It's hard work but then you have to work hard for the things you want in life. It's never straight forward or easy."

His words echoed in my head and I realised if I wanted to get what I wanted I would have to make him see me as a woman and not a child I would have to work at it. He reached out and gave me the money and I took it then retreated to my room.

The next day I was up and out at the crack of dawn to go into the city, I told our driver, an ex-soldier than I would need him for the most part of the day and luckily he had no other plans. I headed first the most exclusive tailor in the city. They had all the latest materials imported from all over the Roman Empire. I chose a sheer loose toga in a light blue colour and bought a matching broach to fasten it with. The material shimmered in the light and it was by far the most alluring and beautiful garment I had ever owned.

Next I headed for the bathhouse. I took a long soak in one of the baths scented heavily with orange and lilac oil. Then an attendant washed my hair and massaged oil into my skin leaving it feeling soft and subtle. I took a very bold step and I had another attendant rid me of all my pubic hair using a very sharp sinister looking razor. Then my hair was curled with hot irons and dressed on top of my head. For the first time in my life I felt sensual. My skin was practically glowing and I could smell lilac and orange. I sashayed back to the carriage feeling like a new woman. We set off for home.

The sun was only about an hour from setting so I ran to my bedroom and changed into my new Toga. I arranged the material so that it fastened on my right shoulder leaving the curve of my left breast exposed. My makeover gave me a confidence boost and I felt ready to throw my cards on the table. The worst that could possibly happen would be my complete humiliation but if he was sending me away anyway I had nothing to lose.

The house was eerily empty and I quickly scuttled through barefoot to Vincent's quarters. I inched the door open and saw he was sleeping soundly, alone. I smiled and entered the room closing the door softly behind me. There were no windows in his room, it was only lit by two small oil lamps and the light from the red embers glowing in the fire.

Vincent was lying face down on the bed the covers had been kicked off and he was exposed totally before me. His buttocks were taut, golden and begged to be caressed. The dip of his back was crying out for a trial of kisses.

"Vincent." I said his name softly and his head shifted slightly. "Vincent." I repeated and this time he turned his head towards me and allowed his eyes to focus.

"Ginetta, is that you." His eyes widened as he realised it truly was me and he sat up. "Ye gods Gina what are you doing."

"I've come to offer myself to you Vincent."

"Gina you are a child you don't know what you're doing, saying."

I reached up and undid the broach on my shoulder and my whole garment fluttered from my body into a pool on the floor."

"Look at me Vincent, do I look like a child. I am a woman. I have the feelings of a woman."

"You do not want this Ginetta. You deserve better than me."

"I love you Vincent and I have since I was ten years old."

"Ten years old?"

"I saw you in the market and you were my knight in shining armour. I always believed you would rescue me and you did. Please do not turn me away Vincent I don't think I could bare your rejection. Look at me and tell me you don't want me."

"Gina, please."

"Look at me."

He did. His eyes travelled from my face, lingering on my breasts, down my navel, his eyes widened at my latest haircut and then they came back up to meet mine."

"You are beautiful Gina."

I approached the side of the bed beside him.

"Then please take me, I give myself to you completely, heart and soul. You own me and you always will."

I brought my lips to his and at first he did not respond but I ran my tongue lightly over them. At last this awakened him and he returned my kiss bringing his hand up to cup the back of my neck and bringing me closer.

In one fluid motion he stood, towering over me. My eyes drank him in. I brought my fingertips up to touch his chest. It was like steel beneath my fingertips. He seemed content to let me explore, and with a little smile he urged me to carry on. Every muscle on his stomach was defined and I delighted in feeling how solid every inch of him was. My eyes travelled to the part of him I so wanted and so feared. I remembered from the time I had seen him that he was amply endowed but seeing him up close, inches from my fingertips he seemed enormous.

"Are you scared my Gina?" He whispered softly

"Yes but I want to please you so much Vincent, teach me, tell me how to."

"How about I please you, how about I pleasure you so much that the Gods themselves become jealous."

I could not speak, could not find words to answer. He kissed me again, much deeper this time. My passion was ignited tenfold. My fingers found his hair and his hands caressed the small of my back. My head was spinning and I thought if a kiss were so good, how would I cope with anything else?

I was inched back onto the bed slowly while his kisses trailed down my neck. I shivered as he reached the spot where my life force flowed beneath my skin and I had a flash imaged of him taking me completely, drinking me. I sank into the bed and let out a cry and his mouth travelled down and found my nipple. He suckled me gently sending little spasms shooting up my spine. I arched my back and he brought both his hands under the small of my back supporting my tiny waist. My skin tingled and burned beneath his kisses and I could not help but moan and gasp. I had never wanted anything so badly in my life. I wanted to feel every inch of him inside me and each time I felt his ample length knock against my leg it ignited a vixen within me.

"Take me, please."

He chuckled softly, his face a few inches above my belly button.

"Don't make me wait, Vincent I need you." I begged

"I won't make you wait my precious Gina but you need warming a little then you'll be ready."

"I feel like I'm on fire already"

"I don't want to hurt you my lovely. Just lie back and let me do my work."

He gave me a devilishly smouldering look, ran his hands down my legs and grabbed them behind the knees. Then with a cheeky wink his eyes left mine and his head dipped down and he took me in his mouth.

I saw stars. I saw the moon and the Gods. As his tongue touched me, parted me and caressed me I was overcome, tipped over the edge. Something, some strange sensation was building within me. I instinctively grasped his hair to pry him off me but it was like trying to move a boulder. The intensity built and built and when I thought I would explode my body found release. Small waves rolled over me, fierce at first but slowly they ebbed away leaving me gasping and panting.

"My god." I gasped when I was able to speak.

Vincent towered over me once more, smiling at the pleasure he had so generously given me.

"You are simply glowing Gina."

"Am I ready for you?"

He hummed softly into my ear and positioned himself between my legs. I felt his length pressing into me, meeting resistance.

"Are you ok my love?" He stopped and looked at me

"Yes keep going please, don't you dare stop."

He tried again. He seemed impossibly large and I winced as I tried to accommodate him. He pushed in little bursts trying to cause me the least discomfort. Then he suddenly broke through and his entire length was buried deep inside me. I cried out and wrapped my arms around his neck.

He paused to let me catch my breath then he began to pump slowly in and out me all the while caressing my skin with his fingers and mouth. The pleasure was intense, so intense, and the pain of my innocence was mingled in with it. He took it slow and I enjoyed every delicious inch of him over and over again. I loosened my embrace so I could look upon him and I saw that his fangs were bared. He quickly covered them with his lips.

"It's OK," I whispered, "I know about you"

"You know?"

"Yes."

There was a distinctive metallic smell in the air. "Is it the blood?"

"Yes, but it's OK I would never hurt you."

"But I want you to."

He stopped abruptly.

"No Gina, you mean more to me than that."

"I know but I want you to." I brought my hips up to meet his driving him deep within me once more. He groaned in pleasure. I wantonly exposed my neck to and tilted my head full back. He continued his thrusts, faster this time and more urgent. I cried out wanting him deeper still. I felt a familiar feeling building inside me once more but this time I embraced it and as my pleasure was at its peek Vincent sank his fangs into my neck and straight into the welcoming vein. The sensation increased and I collapsed onto the bed. The waves did not subside this time, they pulsated through me over and over again. I became light headed and on the verge of fainting when at last I felt him release himself deep inside me. He withdrew from my neck and planted small kisses there while to my relief and dismay the intensity began to dwindle.

Afterwards I felt so at peace and so complete. We lay there for the longest time wrapped in each other's arms, contemplating the line we had crossed. I was content just to stare into his eyes even though they were creased with concern.

"How long have you known?"

"Since I was fifteen."

He sat up surprised.

"How could you have known for so long, weren't you scared?"

"Not at all, I saw you feeding from Carlina but I also saw the pleasure it brought her. You were my savior, I knew you weren't evil. Is there a name for what you are?"

"A vampire."

"Vampire," I repeated. "And can you not go out in the day."

"No and only blood sustains me, human blood."

"And you have not changed since I saw you that day when I was ten."

"No, I have not changed since the day I was turned over three thousand years ago"

I found it hard to even contemplate a number so large.

"Three thousand years! Have you always lived in Rome?"

"I was turned in this area but I have travelled all over the world. I can only spend so long in one place then I must move on. So what now my lovely Gina?"

"I want to stay here with you."

"Don't you see that you deserve more? Life is so precious Gina. Don't you want children, a husband."

"Maybe but for now my heart wants you. Will you send me away?"

"I will not. If you want to stay here, then this will make me very happy but I feel as though I am robbing you."

I laughed.

"Vincent, but for you I would still be at The Gilded Swan. Let me devote my time to you like I have seen the other girls do."

"You could be so much more my love."

"Shh, this is all I want to be."

Already my body craved him again and to show willing I kissed him. He responded immediately this time with no hesitation. I was more confident and reached down to grasp him.

"Why don't we go bathe and you can tell me where on earth you managed to find such a garment." He looked at my see through toga lying in a pool on the floor.

"I had to arm myself with the best weapons, I was petrified you would reject me."

"I think it worked."

"Will you tell me more about you Vincent, about the real you."

"You have kept my secret for many years Gina, I will tell you anything you wish to know, but I want you to promise me one thing Gina."

"Yes."

"Take your time thinking about this decision. I cannot bear you children, or grow old with you. You must promise me you will consider all options. Spend some time with your mother and think everything through, promise?"

"I promise."

Vincent went and ordered a bath to be run and within ten minutes his large square sunken bath was filled with orange blossom smelling water. I pinned my long tresses up with a metal clip and stepped into the water. Vincent grabbed some lilac soap, joined me and began to wash my shoulders and back.

"Are there many of your kind?" I asked

"Quite a few in the city."

"Really?"

"Yes, most of us aren't savages and we don't go round murdering the locals so we are able to live aside humans in peace."

"Why don't you go out in the sun?"

"It burns my skin." He laughed as I gasped. "Don't look so shocked, I don't burst into flames instantly but it isn't pleasant."

I leaned back into his chest and he enveloped his arms around me

"I wish you would reconsider Gina. My other girls they know what they are signing up for and they get paid well but you my lovely Gina. I feel I am taking away your life."

"You gave me life Vincent."

"You keep saying and now you wish to be a slave once again."

"No I want to be with you, willingly and wholly yours"

"If you stay you must never think that you are tied here, when the time is right I want you to go and know that you have my blessing."

"Yes Vincent."

I was in absolute bliss as Vincent walked me to my chambers and gave me a lingering kiss goodnight. This was the time of night were he worked and I was simply exhausted. I had everything. I had my prince. True I would never have him in the conventional way, as my husband but this wasn't a conventional situation. I had so many questions for him but I was practically falling asleep where I stood.

"Get some sleep my lovely Gina and I will see you tomorrow night."

I gave him one last hug and entered my bedroom. I crawled beneath the covers and within minutes was asleep dreaming of Vincent once more.

I awoke as the bright sunlight caressed my face through my window. I stretched and winced at the pain between my legs. The wince was soon replaced by a huge smile. I really was a woman now and I wanted Vincent to show me, teach me everything there was to know about lovemaking.

I lay quietly for a few more minutes remembering the night before feeling my body awaken again. I was also ravenous, so shaking naughty thoughts from my head I dressed and headed to the kitchen to eat and begin my day's chores. Marvette was preparing bread dough.

"Good morning child" Marvette greeted me warmly.

"Morning. Here I can do that."

She wagged her aged finger at me.

"Not anymore." She smiled.

"Why?"

"I had a visit from Master Vincent last night."

"Oh." I hid my smile… badly.

"Yes I can't deny that I wanted more for you Gina love."

"I love him Marvette."

"I know you do. I have seen the way your eyes follow him. I thought you would grow out of it. He told me to instruct you to spend a few days with your mother and think things through."

"That is a really good idea, I would like to see mama for a few days."

"You are simply glowing child but are you sure that being one of the Masters ladies is enough for you?"

"Marvette I love him with my heart and soul. I don't think I've ever felt so alive and happy."

"Well that's all that matters. Now you go sit at the table and I'll bring you breakfast. Perhaps you can be the one to tame him, I have to admit there was a twinkle in his eye as he told me."

"This won't change me MayMay. I'd rather eat here with you like I always have, now give me that dough."

She laughed and shook her head at me.

"I'll make us some lemon tea."

"Lovely."

After the cooking was done for that days meals and the kitchen was clean I decided to go for a walk on the grounds before heading out to see my mother. The grounds of Vincent's Villa were breath taking and I never tired of walking within them, delighting in all the exotic plants he had ordered but he had never seen in the sunlight as they were meant to be seen. I picked an orange from a nearby tree and began to peel it as I walked.

"I don't believe it Carlina!"

I stopped, and ducked behind a bush out of sight. Sitting on a bench in the middle of the garden were Carlina and one of the other girls sat side by side.

"I went to his chamber last night" Carlina sounded angrier than I had ever heard her before. "Imagine my disgust when he told me he'd already fed. Then he announces bold a brass that SHE is joining his little harem."

"I didn't think he went for them so young."

"He doesn't I've been here the longest and I've seen a fair few come and go and they are never so young. He likes us to be experienced."

"So what's the fascination with her then?"

"He bought her from The Gilded Swan years ago. She was *the* help."

"Really?"

"Yes but he took a shine to her, spent hours teaching her all sorts of nonsense. I am so angry. If she thinks she can replace me…."

"Calm down Carlina. Look we girls all know what Vincent likes and no one knows better than you ok. So what do you think he's going to choose, a virgin who knows nothing of the ways of the body or you who knows him inside out intimately?"

"You are right. I'm worried over nothing. Vincent loves it when I take control. I'll make him crave me just wait and see."

"Come let's eat I think I smelt the old hag baking sweet bread."

I was angry at the referral to Marvette as a Hag. She had served them all for years and years and never complained. I waited till they were well out of sight then I made my way to the bench and sat.

Carlina was right. Despite being horrible and seeing me as a threat she was right. I knew nothing about sex. If I wanted Vincent to love me the most then I needed to learn everything there was to know about the way of the body. I thought and thought but there really was only one person I could think of that could help me.

Chapter Six

An hour later I stood outside The Gilded Swan. I wanted to try to find the whereabouts of my only friend there, Anazia. I knew her service to Maricius was over but I was hoping to bribe him into telling me where she resided.

I found Colette behind the bar serving drinks to the afternoon patrons enjoying their lunch. She seemed not to have changed. Her frame was still heavy set and her hair was tied up on top of her head. She seemed a lot happier than I remembered.

"Hi Colette." I said shyly.

"Good lord, I didn't think I'd see your face again child."

"I did not think you would remember me I was here only a short time."

"Ah but you are the one that got away." she laughed. "Maricius was infuriated for months. It was hilarious."

"He's not here?" I said slightly worried. "I mean I don't want to make him angry."

"He's not here, he died last year." She said it without a hint of remorse.

"I'm sorry."

"Don't be, I'm not. He angered the wrong person and met the business end of a dagger.

"How awful."

"For him yes. Now everything is mine. I deserve it too. I ran this place for years, bore him four children while he went through dozens of the working girls."

It sounded harsh but she was right. In my short time at The Gilded Swan I could not deny that Colette was a hard worker. I simply nodded.

"This can't be a social visit."

"No I was trying to track down my friend who used to work here. Anazia, could you help me find her."

She laughed.

"That won't be too hard at all she's asleep in her room in the back."

"She's still here!"

"Oh yes. She served her two years and she decided to stay on. She's our highest earner. She could leave here tomorrow and take with her enough money to see her through till she's dead and gone."

"I don't believe it."

"She only has one client as well at the moment. A wealthy Roman prefect stationed in Egypt of all places. He comes every few weeks and she goes to stay with him at his Villa. He pays her and us generously so that no other man touches her."

"Good gods."

"Go through and see her. She is in the last bedroom near the gates to the garden, you remember the way?"

"Yes. Thank you Colette."

"No problem child. I knew when I first saw you that you were destined for a different path."

I smiled and went through to the kitchen. Memories began flooding back, some good ones where Anazia was making me laugh and blush at her brazenness and bad ones, mainly the fear of what I was going to have to do.

I made my way through the kitchen to the girl's quarters and I gave my old bedroom door a good once over. I wondered who slept there now. At last I came to Anazia's bedroom door. I knocked softly.

"Who is it?" Came a sleepy reply.

"It's Ginetta."

"Ginetta?" There was a pause, "Ginetta! Come in, come in"

I opened the door slowly. Her bedroom was huge with lots of very expensive furniture with gold inlay. It all looked very foreign and exotic and I wondered if these were gifts from her prefect.

I lingered in the doorway. The bed she was laid upon was as big as Vincent's and was covered in exotic animal furs.

"I don't believe it Ginetta." She said warmly.

"Hi"

"Come in, come in."

I took a small step inside.

"Gods Gina, you're as shy as ever get the hell in here."

I laughed and entered properly closing the door behind me and approaching her on the bed.

"I can't believe your still here." I said.

"Are you kidding? I love it here. I've got more jewels and money than I could shake a stick at."

"You do seem happy."

"I am. And look at you Gina you look so beautiful. I missed you after you left. We didn't really get the chance to spend a lot of time together. I wish you could have seen my debut night. I missed you."

"I know. I'm sorry I didn't come and see you, truth be told I was petrified of this place."

"I understood. Boy was Maricius mad as hell when you left. How was your new home."

I proceeded to tell Anazia all about Vincent adopting me, teaching me. I left out his secret of course but did fill her in on the previous nights activities.

"So I have everything I wanted." I added. "But I want him to desire me like no other."

"Ahh I'm getting it. So you came to the only person you knew enjoyed bedroom antics."

"Well yes... sorry."

"Don't be," she laughed. "You're in luck. Quintus is not due back for another few weeks so I have plenty time on my hands."

"How do you do it?" I said in awe, "I do not want to offend but how is it that you have a Roman prefect so besotted with you that he pays so no other man touches you."

She laughed heartily.

"Gina, I'm not offended. Men are easy creatures to overcome because they think with their manhood first then their heads second. I give Quintus what he gets nowhere else and while I'm able to do that, he won't want any other man getting it. He has even talked about marrying me and taking me to Egypt"

"Wow"

"I know. It would be as a second wife but still."

"Wow, do you think you will."

"Probably but I don't let him think I'm too interested."

"Why?"

"You have so much to learn Ginetta." She laughed at my puzzled expression.

In a single graceful motion she stood up out of the bed completely naked. She looked every bit as exotic as the last time I had seen her in all her finery and I could not help but admire her brazen attitude. I wished at that moment that the gods would give me the strength to get my man. I wanted Vincent to desire me, not just appreciate that I was pretty. I wanted him to want me above all others.

Anazia padded to a chest in the corner of the room and pulled out a silk robe that looked as if it had cost a small fortune and it probably had. She tied the robe at the waist, slid her feet into some matching sandals and led me out into the small courtyard where we had spoken all those years before. She seemed to have matured so much to me and in her presence I felt like a small child.

We sat on a marble bench and she plucked a blossom from a nearby tree and inhaled its fragrance deeply. Each movement she made no matter how small and insignificant was graceful and sexy.

"You look so scared Ginetta."

"I am, I won't lie."

"Gina, men are simple to manipulate and control. By the time I'm finished with you he will dismiss his other woman and it will be only you. Until Quintus returns I will do my best to teach you, you can stay with me here."

"Here!"

"As a guest Gina just a guest."

"I know but still."

"I am going to teach you how to walk, talk and breathe like a goddess."

"Thank you." I breathed, relishing the thought.

"Don't thank me yet, you've got a lot to learn."

We chatted some more and I left to fetch some belongings from home in order to begin my teachings.

Once home, I gathered up some of my nicer clothes I had acquired while I'd stayed with Vincent. I left a loving note for Vincent saying I was doing as he instructed and visiting my mother. I wanted all the other details of my time away from the villa to remain secret.

I hopped back in the carriage and began my journey back into the city. I had a lot of time to think about my life. I know to an outsider my actions might have seemed ludicrous, after all Vincent had offered me enough money to be independent for the rest of my days. In a time where all women desired marriage and children I only desired Vincent. If I had to settle for sharing him then it would have to be enough. Somewhere along the way the old Gina, the child disappeared and the woman within me that loved and desired emerged fully by the time I arrived back at The Gilded swan. I felt ready to learn and embrace everything that Anazia wanted to teach me.

The following days were fascinating and embarrassing. Anazia threw herself into teaching me everything she knew…everything. I absorbed everything like a sponge and when it came to demonstrations, well she saved me the embarrassment of showing me things on a real man instead she used a metal phallus. I still cringe to this day thinking of myself practising on that stupid thing but I was willing to do anything. And if a woman who had captured the heart of such a prominent Roman told me to practice on a phallus, I was going to do it.

She taught me how to make the smallest of movements graceful and how to carry myself to make my body movements more alluring. She made me practise over and over again until everything became second nature. My hips swayed differently when I walked. I reached differently for my goblet and Anazia even taught me to speak in a more alluring manner. I could see and feel all these subtle changes, they boosted my confidence.

One night we sat in her bedroom on a fur rug in front of her fire.

"Now I've taught you about how to please a man but you need to embrace your sensuality Gina, you clam up with the mere mention of a penis."

I visibly flinched as she said so brazenly.

"See! Gina, you need to become a sexual creature, let your body guide you. Look, close your eyes."

Trusting her I rose up to my knees and did as she instructed.

I waited with baited breath and was shocked when I felt her lips gently touch mine.

"Don't shy away Gina, embrace it."

I fought the urge to turn my face away and I felt her lips caress mine once more.

I didn't have much to compare it to but her kiss was so soft compared to Vincent's. I felt her hands at my waist and expertly undid my stolla letting it flutter to the floor. I held my ground. Her lips left mine and gently encased one of my nipples in her mouth. She gently flicked it to a firm peek all the while caressing my back and bottom with her hands.

I felt my body responding to her gentle touch, felt myself awakening and boldly I reached for her and opened my eyes.

She smiled and gently cupped my cheek.

"So beautiful Gina." She whispered.

We both leaned in to kiss and this time I let myself enjoy it. I revelled in the softness of her full lips and I brought my hand up to her breast, cupping it gently and squeezing it softly. She moaned softly and I felt moisture pool in between my legs.

We kissed for a time, discovering each other and I allowed my hands to explore her back, breasts and bottom. Her skin was smooth and so soft.

She broke away.

"See it's within you Gina, you are a sexual creature. Look you are glowing."

"I never thought I would want a…"

"A woman?"

"Yes."

"Being with a man is one thing, being with two men is outstanding. Being with a woman is different altogether. A woman is naturally sensual and when you put the two together something magical happens."

I was embarrassed that the thought was making me feel so hot and I felt my cheeks blush red.

"Do not feel you are betraying your man Gina, should he know that you were with another woman the very thought would drive him mad with desire."

I nodded.

"I think you arc ready to return little Gina, that fire in your groin," She reached a hand between us, touched me where I was wet with desire, "use it, feed on it. Let it guide you. Ignore your heart let your desire guide you to get your man."

The next day I packed my belongings. I had had my eyes well and truly opened to the ways of the world but I was glad and grateful.

It was with a lot of uncertainty that I left Anazia but my time was up I was going home. I had stored in my head everything I needed and Anazia gave me parting advice.

"Quintus loves the smell of orange blossom in my hair, it's irresistible. Find Vincent's and make sure you use it."

I already knew what Vincent's favourite fragrance was and it certainly didn't grow on a blossom tree, it flowed through my veins.

When I arrived back at the Villa it was dusk and dinner was being served. I entered the dining room to find Vincent at the head of the table and the seats surrounding him taken up by the other women. Carlina threw me a look that could kill.

"Ginetta!" Said Vincent warmly, "you have returned."

I had only been gone a short time but I had changed so much it felt like a year since I'd last seen him.

"Yes I wondered if I might join you."

This small question was hugely significant, it was me asking permission, not only to join the dinner table but also to join his harem, to commit myself fully. He smiled warmly and indicated to an empty place three seats down. I filled my plate with fruit and waited for the right moment.

"So Gina how was your visit?"

"It was nice, I spent a lot of time with my mother and reconnected with a friend I hadn't seen in a long time."

"I missed you." He said warmly.

"And I you Vincent."

Carlina cleared her throat loudly.

"Would pass the wine Ginetta dear?"

She had obviously asked to interrupt our conversation but she had unwittingly given me the opportunity I had needed. In the carriage on the way home I had removed a spare broach from my bag and slipped it into my toga. I quickly removed it and pricked my finger under the table.

"Of course Carlina."

I stood, and pretended I was scratching my neck beneath my hair but I left I thin trail of blood from my ear down a little. I lifted the wine, walked up and obliged Carlina who was sitting right beside Vincent. As I poured I lifted my hair and exposed my neck to him. I heard him inhale, I had barely placed the jug back on the table when, with a motion so fast, Vincent was up from his seat and was kissing me. I responded opening my mouth and caressing his tongue with my own. He then trailed kisses down my neck and lightly licked the area I had dabbed my blood. I brought my finger, which was still bleeding a little up and placed it in his mouth. He shut his eyes and suckled for a few seconds. His eyes met mine and I saw the passion ignite within them. I forgot where we were, I forgot there were other girls at the table. Vincent swept the table with one hand sending goblets flying and he placed me down. He gripped my hair pinning me to the table, I removed my finger from his mouth and entangled both my hands in his hair.

He kissed me again, frenzied and hot, while he fumbled for the opening to my toga. The next thing his fangs were in my neck and he was inside me, all the way inside me to my heart and soul. I lost control and I cried out sending whatever was left on the table flying in all directions. I heard the snorts from the other girls and the scraping of chairs. I kept my eyes shut and focused on Vincent pounding me furiously. It was over before I had found my release but I knew Vincent had not had his fill of my blood or of me.

I smiled warmly as his weight sagged onto me slightly.

"Gina I'm sorry my love."

I smiled, held a finger up to his lips and quieted him.

He stood and held a hand out to help me up. I took it but as I became vertical a horrible dizziness washed over me and my knees buckled.

"I took too much," Vincent's voice was choked full of concern as he scooped me up in his arms and carried me out of the dining room.

I heard Carlina snort that I was obviously faking the whole thing and chatter broke out in the dining room.

I was carried softly all the way through to my bedroom where he laid me gently on the bed.

"You leave me and return as a temptress my beautiful Gina. Are you Ok my love?"

"Yes, I have not eaten very much that's all you barely took any at all really."

"Well wait here."

He left and returned seconds later with a plate laden with fruit and some sweet bread.

"Will you stay Vincent?" I asked as he laid the plate beside me and joined me on the bed.

"Of course and you shall tell me if you have had a pleasant time away from the villa."

Chapter Seven

I didn't like to hide any truth from Vincent but I couldn't very well tell him I had deliberately left to school myself in the art of sex. I was highly embarrassed to think of it myself. I brushed my doubt aside and told him how happy my mother was and how nice it had been to spend time with her. This wasn't a lie, I had seen my mother often in my brief stay with Anazia and she was positively glowing. She had tried desperately to see if she could locate my father and two brothers but she had had no luck. No records were ever kept of the handover of slaves, soldiers simply ransacked a village or town and captured them. It was very unlikely that my family was even still alive, as being a male slave was crippling work and accidents happened often as they did the most dangerous work of anyone.

I snuggled into Vincent as I told him of my adventures.

"Did it not make you want to stay with your mother?"

"No, my heart is here with you."

"Gina you are so young and innocent it simply takes my breath away."

His hand found my hair and he toyed idly with my tresses.

"Although I am beginning to think maybe not too innocent." He smiled and kissed the top of my forehead. "So what now my lovely Gina."

"I want to spend the night entwined in your arms. I want to rain down upon you all the love I have hidden all these years."

"That sounds painful." he joked and I tapped him playfully on the chest.

"I'm serious Vinnie, I want to be totally exhausted by sun-up and then I want to spend the entire day asleep entwined in your arms."

"Well I usually sleep alone Gina."

"I know but you can make an exception."

He smiled at my forwardness and shrugged his shoulders in agreement.

"Sounds like a plan."

I shifted my weight and reached my head up to kiss him. He returned it sending little electric sparks shooting all over my body. I moaned softly and reached down under his toga, grasping him firmly in my hand.

He growled as I worked him as I had expertly been shown and then, breaking away from his kiss I crawled my way down and took him in my mouth. Suddenly all the embarrassing moments where worth it as I heard Vincent gasp and cry out as I milked him, kneaded him and swirled my tongue around his tip. I got him really wet and used both my hands, one twisting firmly round his shaft and the other kneading his sack. I gave a silent cheer as he released himself just moments later.

"In the name of god Gina where did you learn such a thing?"

"Did you enjoy it?"

"Couldn't you tell, I've never spent myself so quickly."

'Thank you Anazia' I silently thought.

"Well I expect the favour returned."

"Really?" he raised his eyebrow

"Yes, really."

He laughed softly then did as I commanded.

After I had been driven to the edge of ecstasy and back we fell asleep and slept the whole day through entwined in each other's arms. Then I never really left. I spent every day entwined there and he never once asked for the solitary sleeping time I knew he had always demanded. For the next month I was content to shut the day away completely. I fed Vincent as often as I could but I could not solely sustain him. It truly broke my heart when he fed on one of the other girls but he never stayed away long. We walked hand in hand in the gardens basking in the moonlight. We made love under the stars and I forgot everything else.

"You seem deep in thought my lovely." I said one evening as we lay naked on a fur rug in front of the huge roaring fire in his bedroom.

"I got an invitation delivered this morning. I've been invited to a very important Gala Party across town."

"That sounds lovely, so why do you look so troubled."

"I often attend these things but I have always taken Carlina with me."

"Oh." I tried to keep a straight face. "Vincent you don't have to feel guilty, if you want to take Carlina it's fine. I will be here when you come back."

"No, you misunderstand me my love. I wish you to accompany me, I just know I have to let Carlina know."

"Oh." I kept my face serious but inside I was simply glowing. We were going away together, just the two of us. We would be out in public looking and behaving like a normal couple.

He bent his head down and took one of my nipples in his mouth. I hissed and brought my fingers to his hair. He suckled me for a moment then laid his head on my stomach, looking up at me with his piercing blue eyes.

"I wish I could make you happy Gina."

"Vincent, I've never been more happy."

"I never gave much thought to love before. Never wanted or felt the need to find my soul mate."

"Soul mate?"

"We don't fall in love like humans Gina. A vampire is drawn to an individual human, and if they feel the same they are soul mates. I have a friend in the city that found his soul mate and he says it's the most wonderful feeling. I look at you Gina and I can imagine being human with you. You make me long for something more and yet I am helpless to act on it."

"Oh Vincent. If you turn me we can still be together as we are now."

"That's the sad thing. Vampires do not interact with each other like that."

"Never?"

"Never, unless they are soul mates."

"So if you turn me you won't want me."

"No my love, and you will not want me either."

"I can't imagine it" I said shocked.

"It's true, I wish in my heart of hearts that we were soul mates."

His words made my heart soar. I loved him and if I could only love him as a human than I was content to die loving him.

"It doesn't matter Vincent, just love me until..."

"Don't Gina"

"It's true though, I will age, and then you won't desire me anymore. It's fine."

"You make me sound like a monster, but it's how I have lived for so long. I am only now seeing it in a different light."

"Let us talk of something else Vincent."

"What my love?"

"Tell me about when you were human. What was it like all those years ago?"

"I never actually lived among humans. I was bred to be a vampire."

"A slave?"

"I suppose so yes. There had been a great vampire war and our numbers had been severely depleted. The packs left, captured humans, bred them and trained the children to become warriors. The strongest and the most resilient were turned when they became men."

"Resilient?"

"It wasn't ideal. Vampires don't usually have compassion for humans. We were pitted against each other from an early age, beaten, ridiculed. We never lacked food because we were needed to be as healthy as possible."

"Gods, I thought I'd had a hard child spending those years with Augustus."

"It's all I knew. I was turned in my twenties and I was a true warrior, entering the battlefield with vigour and no fear."

"All the shields and swords on the walls?"

"From all my victories. I made my way up to general and was a trusted member of my pack. I loved and still do, a good battle. The smell of victory is a rush."

"You sound so passionate when you speak about it."

"It is nice to be able to speak freely and have someone who is interested in listening."

"I love listening to you Vincent, I always have."

He chuckled.

"I could never understand how you could listen to me prattle on for so long when your tutoring began."

"I enjoyed every moment."

"And to think you knew what I was."

"Yes."

"How could you not say anything."

"I was afraid you would send me away if I told you I knew."

"You need not worry about that now my love."

"I know, I love you Vincent." I said with sincerity.

"And I love you Gina, more than I thought I possibly could love a human."

Chapter Eight

I was ecstatic that Vincent had chosen me, me and only me to accompany him to the grand party. We would stay in a grand palace and to all eyes we would be a loving couple. His words were playing around in my head from the previous night. He loved me more than he had loved any human, he wished I were his soul mate. It was enough. I adored him enough for both of us. I never wanted to leave him, although inevitably I knew I would have to, death or old age would take me away from him.

I had a few days to prepare so I ordered a new garment for the occasion. It was a dress of deep red with gold trim and a low bust, very daring for the time but I wanted to do Vincent justice. I skipped merrily through the house and Marvette laughed at my enthusiasm.

"My dear child you are simply glowing."

"It's love Maymay, love." I took the dusting cloth from her and began dancing and singing as I worked. It was infectious and soon Marvette was singing alongside me.

"You are changing master Vincent too." She said when we were both exhausted.

"How?" I asked with curiosity.

"He is softer, he smiles more."

"Really?"

"Yes silly, he obviously loves you too, its time he ditched those hussies and made an honest woman of you."

"I don't think that will happen Marvette but what I have is enough."

"I hope so my dear."

I helped to knead bread, ground some flour, tenderised meat and any other little jobs that Marvette needed. I was so happy I was fit to burst but of course it wasn't to last. After lunch I went to collect all the linens from the other girls for washing. Even though I was now their equal, even more so as I often stayed with Vincent right through the day, something which none of the other girls got to do, I still collected their linens and stoked their fires. I did for Maymay. When I reached Carlina's I knocked softly.

"Carlina, it's Ginetta, do you have any linens for the maids to wash?"

"Two seconds, OK come in."

She'd thrown a thick blanket around herself and took a seat by the fire. She didn't motion to help me strip the bed. I didn't care.

"You know when Vincent brought you home I laughed." She said frostily

I stopped what I was doing and turned to face her.

"I even thought that your crush on him was hilarious. Your little puppy dog eyes would follow him everywhere and it was childish. I thought twice when he started to bed you, after all you are younger than I, but I have been favoured for nearly ten years and I told myself not to worry."

My breath caught in my chest as I waited for her to continue.

"However last night I was told that Vincent was going to the most prominent party in Rome and he was taking you, not I."

"Carlina I,"

"What!" She hissed, "You're sorry, no you aren't sorry."

"I can't help loving him." I whispered

"It's not love, you idiot. You are obsessed with him and it's pathetic.

"What do you want from me?" I said getting slightly irritated now.

"I will pay you"

"Beg your pardon?"

"I'll pay you. I will give you all my savings to leave here."

"I don't want your money."

"You can't stay here forever, take it now and leave us alone."

I was speechless. I didn't care if she were offering me the treasures of Rome herself, I wasn't leaving Vincent's side. I turned my back on her.

"Strip your own god damned bed." I said calmly and with that I slammed the door on her.

I simply avoided her the next few days, which wasn't easy considering she took every opportunity to bitch and whine really loudly how much she hated me. Marvette even threatened to speak to Vincent, but I forbade her. I didn't need the situation making any worse, and besides Vincent and I were to be leaving for the big party soon. My dress was ready and the carriage was packed for our departure.

Marvette waved us off with the biggest smile on her face and I waved from the carriage all the way down the road

we were out of sight. I snuggled up into Vincent's arm and enjoyed it being the two of us, out in public, together. I still couldn't believe it.

"Gina if you smile any wider, I swear you'll do yourself an injury."

"I'm so happy Vinnie."

"I could make you happier. I have news for you."

"What?"

"I've been thinking, Gina. Since you came into my life I've been so happy, you've made me feel almost human again with your warmth and love. I meant what I said the other night. I wish so much that we could be soul mates but if I cannot give you that then I want to give you the next best thing."

"What are you saying Vincent?" I could barely contain myself.

"When we return I will be dismissing the other girls, I will still have to feed once or twice a week elsewhere but I want to give you this."

"So it will be just you and I?"

"Yes Gina"

I threw my arms around him and squeezed him tight.

"Oh Vincent, I will make you happy!"

"You already do my sweet." he returned the embrace just as eagerly then kissed me so tenderly. I couldn't believe it, all my dreams had come true. My dream man was mine, all mine.

The place where the party was being held could only be described as a palace. The pillars at the front loomed over us. Guards stood outside to great us and lead the carriage away to the stables, and then an older gentlemen stood at the top of the stairs to check us off the guest list.

We were then guided through to our bedroom to prepare for the party ahead and I was relieved to see our room, while extremely lavish only had one small window, which we would easily be able to cover.

"The room is lovely Vincent." I told him

"Only the best for you Gina, I'd say we have a little time before we need to get ready, what would you like to do?"

"Hmm, let me think?" I smiled because even as I said it he was unpinning my broach and relieving me of my clothing.

"Gina, your skin is delectable."

I gasped as his fangs nipped the tender flesh of my breast but I ran my fingers into his hair to encourage him.

"Turn around and grab the bed post."

I followed his command without question. He pulled my hair to one side and licked the skin below my earlobe. I shivered. Already wet with desire for him I rubbed my bottom against him.

"Like a little kitten my Gina, you almost purr."

"Take me, please."

He laughed softly at my impatience but I felt him quickly remove his clothes and then felt the coolness of his chest pressing into my back. He entered me slowly, deliberately keeping me waiting. I groaned as I felt him fill me. His hands kneaded my breasts as he began his slow masterful strokes, touching my core. One of his hands worked its way down and he stroked me in time. I felt a familiar sensation building and cried out his name over and over. My hair was quickly moved aside and his fangs were in my neck, drawing my life force, which I gave so willingly. I felt myself pulsating around him and my legs nearly buckled beneath me. He joined me and I relished his seed planted deep within me. He suckled a little more then scooped me up and placed me on the bed where we lay until we were fashionably late.

As I dressed in all my finery a little while later I'd never felt happier. I wanted to shout from the rooftops that I felt on top of the world.

He was to surprise me even further. He came to collect me so that we could go to the party and he was carrying a small wooden box. He handed it to me and smiled at my most puzzled expression.

I opened it slowly and was stunned. Inside was a necklace, a gold necklace with the biggest ruby I had ever seen inlaid in the middle.

"Oh Vincent, it's magnificent."

He lifted it out and I turned around so he could fasten it around my neck. I felt the sheer weight of the stone as he let it fall and it rested just above my breasts.

"Shall we go my queen?"

I smiled and took his hand as he led me to the party.

The main room was absolutely breath taking. Tables had been decked out with the finest material and table wear and everywhere you looked there were servants handing out food and drink from gold platters. The richest of the rich were in that very room and most seemed to know Vincent and greeted him warmly. I hung to his arm and played my part and received several compliments.

We laughed and danced and I was a whirl of happy emotions and I had never seen Vincent smile and laugh so much. Late into the night and quite close to dawn the party was still in full swing and Vincent was chatting merrily to some wealthy Roman governors. I decided I would get some air. I kissed him lightly on the cheek and said I would return promptly. He cupped the back of my head gently and told me we would head back up to our room shortly.

I took a walk in the garden located at the centre of the villa. They had orange and lemons trees growing there and the smell was simply divine. I dreamed of what could be, what the future may hold. I would have many, many, happy years with Vincent. When the time came and I was too old to be with him, I thought that dying as a human with my memories would far outweigh living forever without the chance of ever being with him.

Voices coming from a guardhouse caught my attention and as I came within earshot I stopped to listen.

"The place is surrounded and we have provisions set in place to kill the creature."

"Good, you must make sure it is done properly."

Carlina!

"I hope for your sake you are right about this."

"Of course I'm right, I have fed him for the past ten years, and don't look at me like that, I'm sure you have done worse for money."

I tried to hold my breath. I didn't want to make a noise and give myself away.

"I want the tramp that is with him to suffer do you hear. You can have as much fun with her as you like."

I felt bile rise from my stomach and I fled. As I got back to the main hall two soldiers had approached the table and were chatting to Vincent.

"I was just about to retire gentlemen, can this wait awhile?"

"I'm afraid I must insist."

Vincent stood and saw me. He read the look of pure fear on my face. I ran over to him.

"We have to go, now." I hissed.

He was trying to remain calm and he was doing a far better job than I.

"We need you to come with us too miss."

I turned and noticed other soldiers who had entered the room.

"It's Ok my love, come on."

He took my hand and gave it a gentle squeeze. Several people, those who were not totally inebriated by drink had now stopped to stare as we were led away. They took us to the centre of the garden where we were surrounded by at least a dozen soldiers.

"What is the meaning of this?" Vincent was now sounding seriously annoyed as swords were raised and arrows were pointed at us.

A general stepped forward.

"This might be a just a huge inconvenience for you sir, but we must make sure."

"Make sure of what? What the hell is going on?"

"We have been told that you are a demon, a vampire. I'm afraid I can not have another in my city."

"Another?"

"We have discovered, with the help of an excellent source, three of these hideous demons lurking in our city."

"You are making a mistake gentlemen, I will see you lose your jobs for this." I'd never heard Vincent sound so angry before.

"I don't think it's such a mistake"

Carlina stepped out from behind one of the soldiers. Vincent gasped.

"No." He whispered in shock.

"Yes, my darling yes. They simply wouldn't believe me at first. That is until I led them to a few of your friends. I do believe this is the first time I have seen you lost for words. Would you believe that even after staking three of you, they still want to give you the benefit of the doubt. So I suggested we wait awhile, say until dawn."

"Please let Ginetta go?"

"You should really blame her you know, if not for her we would be tucked up in bed together. Not a care in the world."

The general cleared his throat.

"You say this is the last demon in our city woman?"

"That I know of."

"Good." He gave a nod to one of the soldiers stood to her right and in one swift motion he removed a dagger and drove it into her abdomen. I screamed and hugged myself into Vincent.

"I would say that lying down with a demon is just as bad as being one." The general said coolly. Carlina looked at the wound in her chest spilling blood all over her cream dress. She crumbled to floor and the blood seeped into the gravel. She moved no more.

Vincent said nothing and I thought at that moment we were surely going to die. I sobbed into his chest.

"Hold on tight," I heard him whisper.

I stopped and as soon as my hands clasped around his middle he launched himself into the air and on to the roof.

Chaos erupted below us and as I found my footing I saw a shower of arrows heading straight for us. Vincent turned his back to them and sheltered me. I felt the impact as three hit him and jolted him forward.

"We'll run to the back of the house." He picked me up and slung me over his shoulder. It was then I saw the arrows sticking out of his back and his white toga stained with blood, which was getting worse. He began running along the roof tiles with a speed I didn't know was possible even for him. The arrows kept raining down on us and I screamed as he took another in his arm just inches from my face. It didn't even slow him down, he just kept moving.

I could hear the screeching voice of the general to shoot faster. I tried to look under Vincent's arm and I saw the edge of the building approaching and I knew he wasn't going to stop. I closed my eyes tightly thinking it was better I didn't see. I felt him jump and our weightlessness as we soared through the air. As we began to descent I felt something sharp pierce my side just under my ribcage, I cried as a crippling pain engulfed me and I knew it was an arrow. I reached back to touch it and my fingers came back dripping with my own blood.

Vincent landed with a thud and carried on running. I fought to stay conscious but it was hard, so hard. My vision was becoming blurred and then blackness closed in until my whole body went limp and I passed out.

"Gina, Gina. Please, gods don't take her."

I moaned softly.

"Vincent, is that you." It was an effort to speak, I felt so drained but at least I wasn't in any pain.

"Gina you have to wake, look at me."

My eyelids felt weighted down with cement but I opened them to look at him.

"Where are we?"

"A crypt, the sun was rising; I had to find somewhere quick."

He sat me up and propped me up against the wall. I looked down to see that the arrow had pierced me under my ribcage at the back, it had gone in at an angle and the front was protruding through my sternum. The whole of my beautiful dress was drenched in blood.

"That's a real waste." I said and tried to laugh.

"Don't joke Gina, I can't stop it. I can't pull this out. I'm surprised you aren't dead already."

"Just hold me."

"Gina, your heart beat has slowed down, it won't be much longer unless."

I shook my head.

"No Vincent. I couldn't bear it. I'd never be able to be with you."

"Gina, it won't be like that. You won't feel like that about me. Please I beg you."

I started to cry.

"I don't want to not love you."

"Please." A single tear ran down his cheek. I raised my hand shakily to wipe it away and with a simple nod I gave him permission. I could not bear to see him cry. He did not even need to drain me, so close was I to the end. His fangs came out and tore a hole in his wrist.

"One last kiss." I whispered hoarsely and he obliged. His lips met mine and I felt that familiar jolt. I relished that feeling of wanting him so badly for after I was a vampire I would want him no more. He broke away and pressed his wrist to my mouth.

His blood was like sweet honey and it danced around my mouth. I swallowed mouthful after mouthful and felt a fire burning inside me. The ache built and built and yet I did not want to stop drinking, ever. I could hear my own heart, the beat picking up till it was booming loudly in my chest. Vincent tried to take his wrist away but I held on fast sucking noisily.

"Gina enough."

He pulled away and I began to convulse on the floor.

"Don't fight it Gina, just let it wash over you."

I concentrated on his voice then finally passed out again, my beating heart the last thing I remember hearing as a mortal.

Chapter Nine

I opened my eyes once more and was relieved to find that I was no longer in a crypt but lying on a deep comfy bed. I looked around the room. It was lavishly decorated but I didn't recognise it at all. My head hurt and I was so thirsty. I felt like I hadn't drunk a drop in weeks. I tried to sit up but dizziness overwhelmed me and I collapsed back onto the bed. Then I remembered my wound and reached down. I was wearing a thin nightgown and as I ran my fingers over the area the arrow had penetrated me I was surprised to find the skin was silky smooth with no signs of injury at all.

The door in front of me opened and Vincent breezed into the room. I felt a surprising jolt of desire as I worked my eyes over his perfect features. It became a race between how much I desired him and how thirsty I was. Desire temporarily won. He came and sat on the bed beside me and it suddenly dawned on me that if I still desired him the surely he had managed to save me. I was still human, just weak and dehydrated from my injuries. *Oh joy and rapture,* I thought.

"You are awake. You had me worried then my lovely. I almost thought you hadn't made it."

"You saved me, but how?"

"You drank my blood, don't you remember."

"Yes but…."

"Shh, let me go get your dinner. Just a small amount to start, ok."

I nodded. He left and returned with a silver goblet, he helped me sit up and propped me back against the pillow. As his fingers made contact with my skin it felt as though it awakened beneath his touch. I looked at his face and saw his features in a new light. He was truly beautiful in every way, I had surely not been appreciating him fully before. He handed me the goblet and the instant my nose captured a smell of its contents I forgot everything. It was blood. As I snatched it from his grasp and gulped it down as fast as I could I wasn't even repulsed at myself. My thirst was sated a little and the dizziness in my head faded a little but now I was confused.

"What is going on?"

"Ginetta don't you remember, you were shot at the villa."

"Yes, yes I remember that and the crypt but…"

"You are a vampire now Gina, but don't be afraid I will be here for you always."

"You don't understand, I can't be dead I just can't!"

"Calm down, you are still you."

"But why do I still want you! Even more, even stronger than before!"

"That's impossible." He whispered.

"I'm aching for your touch Vinnie, I need you."

"No… Gods, what have I done?"

"You said I would not desire you once I was a vampire."

"You shouldn't it can only mean…" He took a step back, his eyes filled with pain.

"What?"

"I am your soul mate"

"Oh Vincent, that's wonderful… isn't it?"

But Vincent was shaking his head as if the world were going to collapse around us. He covered his face with his hands and sat at the end of the bed.

"Vincent, you're scaring me."

"How could I have missed it?"

"Missed what?"

"That I was your soul mate, the signs, they were there, but it's usually overwhelming for a human and you lived with me for years before we got together."

"I first saw you when I was ten years old and you have been in my dreams every night since. When you rescued me, I wanted so badly to throw myself at your feet but I knew you thought me a child so I waited."

"It must have been because you were so young."

"But surely this means we can be together?"

"No Gina I don't feel the same way."

"What! But you always said you loved me more than any human."

"Yes Gina, as a human I felt more than I'd ever felt before but you are a vampire. Even now you smell different, you look different."

I began to cry.

"So I am to feel this way… forever."

"Yes," he whispered. "I have doomed you, and there is nothing I can do about it."

Even as spoke, telling me he could never love me, never make love to me again, I still wanted him. I wanted to kiss him and prove him wrong. I couldn't imagine feeling the way I did for a day let alone an eternity.

"We could try? At least try." I said desperately.

"Don't you understand that I want to give that which you desire but I physically can't do it."

"Just kiss me please I beg you."

"Don't Gina please, you will make it worse."

"Please!" I sobbed reaching for his hand. He pulled away and a second he was gone from the room leaving me weeping for the life and love I had lost.

I had calmed down to a degree when he returned. I wasn't sure if I'd slept or simply lain looking in to space.

"Are you awake Gina?"

"Yes." I answered without turning.

"I brought you some more blood."

I sat up by myself and took the goblet, again draining it in seconds.

Then I looked at my prince and words tumbled from my mouth, words I couldn't have ever imagined saying to him.

"I need to leave here, I need to leave you."

"I was thinking the same." He saw my hurt expression, "for your own sake."

"I will go as soon as my strength returns."

"You cannot just wander into the world. You are a dangerous predator. You would kill your own mother if she walked through that door."

"My mother! Oh my mother, what will become of her?"

"I will make sure she is taken care of for the rest of her life, but you can't see her Gina."

"Never?"

He shook his head.

"This just gets worse. So what will you do with me Vincent? Lock me away until I can play with the humans."

I was angry now and didn't even disguise the venom in my voice as I spoke. I gasped as I felt a pain in the roof of my mouth and my fangs pushed my incisors out. I hissed at him. Vincent ignored it.

"I have a friend, he has a small pack of vampires. I will contact him and you could go stay with him. Learn what you need to know."

"I hate you!" I screamed

"Gina I wish you did, it would be easier, so much easier."

"Get out! Get out and don't come back till you are ready to shove me out the door and move in the next Carlina!"

He didn't see any point in arguing, I had gone past the point of rational conversation. He turned, shut the door and left me alone once more.

I lay in that bed and I cursed everyone and everything I'd ever known. I slept and dozed and cried for days, or so it seemed. Vincent snuck in while I was sleeping and placed my blood on the side table.

I was hurt that he didn't even want to try to love me. I felt as though my sole existence was to adore him and he couldn't even bear to kiss me. What hurt the most was that he wanted to send me away, he wanted the easy option. I was a new vampire and I had no idea what was expected of me or the sort of creature I would become in the big wide world, but I knew that Vincent didn't want to be my teacher.

The night I had been dreading finally came. I heard Vincent's voice calling me softly, waking me from restless sleep.

"Ginetta, the carriage is here."

I bolted up from the bed and stared at him with wild eyes.

"So you are sending me away?"

"I thought it's what you wanted"

"No!" I shrieked, "I want you to take me in arms and say you'll try to love me. Am I so hideous a creature that you can't even bear to be in the same room as me, you have to sneak blood in while I'm asleep?"

"I cannot love you. I cannot!" He was trying to remain calm but this was making me even more angry.

"Will not, more like."

"Gina?"

"Get out while I dress. The sight of me naked will surely make you vomit now."

He shrugged his shoulders in utter defeat and left.

The trunk at the foot of my bed contained several togas and exotic dresses and I chose a simple slip dress. There was no reason for me to look nice now, it was hopeless.

A soft knock on the door a few minutes later told me Vincent had returned to escort me. I opened the door and followed behind him in silence. We seemed to be in another villa, much smaller than the one I had called home.

As we exited through the front door I saw an ebony coloured carriage with heavily draped windows. The driver approached and greeted Vincent warmly.

"All ready?" He asked

"Yes, are you settling at Damien's?"

"Very well thank you sir."

"Good, good, give my regards and sincere thanks."

He then turned to me.

"I am truly sorry. I hope one day you can return to me Gina and not feel the pain you feel now. I want you to promise me one thing?"

"Why should I promise you anything?"

"For the years we spent together, for the love we shared. Promise me that you will keep in touch. Send word or letter to me through Damien, the pack leader and it will get back to me."

It was cruel but I didn't give him an answer. I wanted so badly to throw myself on him and beg him to try. I wanted it so much it hurt, but instead I followed the driver and got into the carriage and we drove away without a backwards glance.

We stopped after a few hours and the driver climbed into the carriage and offered me a flask.

"It's about as fresh as it can be, give it a shake before you open it."

I took the flask and did as he'd instructed. As I popped off the cap the familiar intoxicating smell of blood hit my nostrils and I started to gulp it down.

"Whoa there, save some for me please."

My eyes widened in surprise.

"You're a…"

"Yes, know how you can tell?"

"How?"

"If I were human you'd have pounced by now, now come on share." He smiled

Under normal circumstances I would have found him very attractive. He had dark silky black hair, slicked back with some type of oil and his skin was darkly tanned.

"What's your name?" I asked handing over the flask.

"Horaldo, and you are Ginetta, the new vampire."

"How long have you been…"

"Around a hundred years, I am a young vampire by our standards."

"And this Damien?"

"Old, older than Vincent and old enough that when he says travel across the land to pick up some new vampire, I do it without question."

"Where are we going?"

"Gallia Transalpina, there is much destruction from the wars but we seem to have faired ok. We have a large house on the outskirts of the city that has seen little damage."

"Vincent had told me how wide spread the Romans are becoming."

"It seemed those who oppose them fair not well. We try not to involve ourselves in human matters."

"Will we reach it before night fall?"

"Heavens no, but we have enough safe houses to get us their safely, it should take around a week."

"A week!"

"Yes, but worry not. We will bed down during the day at the inns we can use safely and travel through the night. I will make sure you are adequately fed. We only have to keep you away from humans."

"Only?"

"Don't look so worried."

Gallia Transalpina was the area of Europe now known as France. Romans had different names for all the areas of Europe during the Gaul wars.

We soon resumed our journey and rode until the sky had started to lighten. I was getting slightly worried that we wouldn't make it in time but soon after we pulled into a very nice looking inn at the side of the road. He instructed me to stay put while he went to enquire about a room.

We were in luck.

It was quiet as my feet hit the dirt of the road and instantly a new smell hit my nostrils and I sniffed the air. To me it smelt like the sweetest sugar bread and it made me so thirsty that I instantly wanted to seek out the source.

Horaldo grasped my arm.

"Stay with me Ginetta and focus on my voice. We access our room round the back of the inn so we shouldn't come across anyone, but I shall hold onto your arm just in case."

I nodded, but that smell, it was like a thousand angels calling me, tempting me.

"Talk to me Horaldo, distract me."

"What shall we talk about?"

We began our walk.

"When you greeted Vincent, I got the impression that you had already met him."

"Indeed I have, he rescued me. I most certainly wouldn't be here if he had not intervened."

"Did he turn you?"

"No, no, I was turned by a lady Vampire. She lured me into her bed and for what ever reason, I will never know, she turned me. She began teaching me the ways of the vampire world and I was slowly adjusting. When I was just a few weeks old however our hiding place was discovered and they killed her. I was torn between the running and feeding. The smell of blood in the air was intoxicating. I chose to run and was being followed by a mob of villagers. I ran across rooftops to avoid capture and I was nearly at the point of exhaustion when Vincent pulled me into his house and hid me.

He couldn't possibly keep me so he asked Damien if he could take me instead and he delivered me himself. He didn't have to do that, most vampires wouldn't have given a damn about a newborn, but he did."

"He couldn't keep you with him because of his lady friends could he?"

"It's true he did have several. Vampires are strange creatures when it comes to feeding. Some, like myself, enjoy the thrill of the hunt, then the seduction. Some vampires enjoy the hunt but enjoy instilling fear in their victims and some, like Vincent, enjoy their meals on tap. It wouldn't appeal to me, I would get bored after a month."

"I was willing to be one, I guess looking back I was one of thousands."

"I don't know very much about Vincent really but I do know one thing."

"What?"

"He hasn't turned anyone for a very, very long time."

"It wasn't the plan," I said fighting back tears, "We were attacked and I was shot with an arrow, he didn't have a choice."

"You are wrong Ginetta."

"What?"

"He could have left you to die. Humans mean very little to us and to him most of his ladies would have been well-pampered food. He put himself in danger by weakening himself to change you and yet he did it."

We reached a gate, which led us into a courtyard. Horaldo led us to one of the doors leading off and I was pleasantly surprised to see a very clean, expensive looking bedroom and sitting room within. I felt simply exhausted and ready to sleep. Horaldo bolted the door and checked the shutters on the windows. He grabbed a fur throw from the bed.

"I will sleep in the sitting area, you can have the bed."

"Thank you." I replied and I crawled under the thick covers and soon I was blissfully asleep.

I dreamt of a different world, a world in which I was human again and Vincent could hold me and love me once more. A world where we lay entwined with each other and our two bodies were as one. I never wanted to wake, I would live forever and I wanted to spend that forever in slumber where I could be his once more.

Horaldo gently shook me awake.

"Good evening." He greeted.

"Evening?" I asked, "Have I slept the whole day away?"

"You give a new meaning to 'sleeping like the dead', you didn't even move once. I have dinner for you. It's pretty fresh."

He handed me a goblet and I gulped my metallic tasting beverage down, wanting more, savoring how it awakened and invigorated me.

"We must get on the road if we want to make good time."

I nodded and followed him to our carriage.

Our journey continued much the same, day after day, night after night, sleeping at various inns. Horaldo was amazing and took such good care of me. I had seen his type in The Gilded Swan. Suave and sophisticated men, good looking and charming to boot and I admit I never would have liked him if I hadn't have been forced to make that journey but I warmed to him. He tended to my every need even ordering me clothes to be delivered when we stayed at one place because I only had the dress I had been wearing when I left Vincent.

After just over a week of traveling the pain in my heart was as raw as ever but without Vincent near me it became manageable. I forced myself not to think of him. I sat by Horaldo and we discussed everything from politics to fashions to keep my mind from wandering back to the inevitable.

While I slept it was different. Every night I dreamt of him and every night it was the same. I was always human and we were always so in love. My heart could not be denied. Part of me welcomed it and part me craved for release from this love I had no control over. I prayed to the gods to give me strength to overcome it and I just hoped they hadn't turned their backs on me, as Vincent had done once I was Vampire.

I was unsure how I felt when Horaldo told me that the next day we would reach Damien's house. I had gotten used to being around him and I was comfortable with him and yet I wanted to be somewhere safe, it was like an inner instinct.

We bedded down for the day in a little village and I awoke expecting Horaldo to have been and got my dinner, as he had every night we had been together.

"I have not been able to get any Ginetta, The brothel was burnt down in a Roman raid and there's naught left."

"A brothel?"

"I have to use the best method possible. These are troubled times, I can't just go round slicing people open and pouring their blood into a flask. I have to be subtle. It's only a few hours to the castle."

"I can't wait that long, please get some."

"Ginetta we can't, there are few people left and those who are, are suspicious. Look you'll be fine but you will need to ride in the carriage until we get there, we can't risk it."

I nodded and held my hands out to see they were already shaking with hunger. I felt parched but water would not quench my thirst.

That ride was horrendous and by the time the carriage came to a stop I was nearly clawing at the walls with hunger. The door had been bolted from the outside and I understood why this precaution was necessary, had anything human come with a few feet of the carriage I would have pounced.

Horaldo opened the door and I saw we had gone to the rear of a large stone building, it reminded me of the cottages and farm buildings from before I was enslaved but this was on a bigger scale. The stone was dark and so different to the white wash plaster of roman villas. I forgot my hunger for the tiniest second to take in the pure beauty of the building before me.

"Come Ginetta, Damien with have blood for you."

"My mind snapped back on track and I eagerly followed"

I was led into a very plain, cell like room with a heavy wooden door and a simple box bed. Horaldo sat me down and joined me. My hands were shaking now and I felt on the point of dizziness.

"Will it always be this way?"

"No Ginetta, as you age you won't need to feed as often. I can skip a day now if need be."

"I feel like I'm going to die!" I gasped and clutched my dry, parched throat.

As if on cue a woman appeared in the doorway carrying a silver goblet on a delicate tray. I jumped off the bed and snatched it, sending the tray flying to the floor.

"Did you feed her at all on your journey Horaldo?"

"Lithia had been ransacked, we were lucky to get room at the inn for shelter."

"Hmmm that's quite close, I will inform Damien. He says she is to rest and he will call on her tomorrow evening."

In the meantime I had drained the goblet in two large mouthfuls and sat back on the bed with pure relief.

"She is a pretty thing, but then Vincent has impeccable taste."

My head snapped up.

The woman had raven black hair and dark smoldering eyes. Her face was lightly tanned and her cheekbones high. She smiled showing me perfect row of white teeth.

"Got your attention young one."

"You know him?"

"Yes, very well, when I was human."

"Is this where he sends all his cast offs?"

"Oh he didn't turn me, refused to but I had ways and means."

I stared openmouthed.

"You will be fine here young Ginetta, once you have your thirst under control you will be given a more adequate room and lodgings for as long as you desire."

"Thank you."

"Come Horaldo, Damien wishes to speak to you before he goes hunting."

"Ok." He turned to me. "Sleep, you are safe now, I will see you tomorrow."

With that they both left, shut the door and locked me inside.

I wept into the darkness, wept for everything I wanted and could never have and as my eyes closed and I succumbed to sleep Vincent's face was the last image imprinted on my mind.

Chapter Ten

A new night and a new home. My eyes opened and for the tiny split second in the haze of coming out of sleep, everything was OK. As my mind fully awoke that sense of dread kicked in and everything came flooding back. It was almost a relief when the overbearing thirst fully kicked in. I lay shaking like a leaf, staring at the cracks in the wall to distract myself.

I heard the bolt slide on the door and I jumped up. It was the woman with the black hair. She held a goblet of blood out for me and smirked slightly as I shot off the bed and drained it in a couple of mouthfuls.

When I was calm she came fully into the room.

"My name is Leanna."

"Ginetta."

"Horaldo and Damien spoke about you last night. Had I known, I might not have been so… brash last night."

"I don't need pity." I said sharply.

"No and you won't get it from me, but I do know what you are going through."

"Did you love Vincent too?"

She laughed and her beautiful face lit up.

"No, but when I left Vincent I fell in love, deeply in love with a Vampire and she felt the same."

"She?"

"You do not choose your soul mate. Phena was a goddess, ancient and deadly. We fell in love and had many happy decades entwined together, making love endlessly."

"So you know how I feel but Vincent does not feel the same."

"I lost Phena last year."

"Oh…"

"They rounded her up, pulled her fangs out as trophies and cut off her head."

"Oh Leanna"

"I need not your pity either. I saw it all; she had hidden me to protect me. She died to save me."

"Does it get easier?"

"Yes but I cry every day. I detest humans for taking her away from me but seven months on I can function."

"I am truly sorry that you lost her. To know that Vincent is alive carrying on without me fills me with such a strong mix of anger and jealously it scares me. I wish him dead, and then know I could never hurt him. I wish he had left me to die, never turned me."

"So you have two choices you can walk out into the sun or you can choose life. Deal with your sorrow and become a productive member of this pack. When the time is right you may choose to leave or like me you might choose to remain. I will never leave this place. My memories are all I have."

She gave me a slight smile.

"You will need to spend a few weeks here we have human servants and slaves and need to protect them. I can however bring you things to amuse you."

I listened to her words and took them in. I needed a sharp reality check. I would never forget Vincent, never stop overwhelmingly loving him but I could make something of my life. I asked Leanna for books. Books were a rare thing at that time and not so easy to come by. But she brought me several, and I began a lifelong passion of collecting books, which I still have to this day.

Later that evening I was paid a visit from Damien. He unbolted my door and stood there. He was smaller than I imagined the leader of a pack would be and he didn't seem to be built like a warrior at all. He looked like he had been turned in his forties and his brown short hair was peppered with grey.

"Good evening, Ginetta."

I stood and bowed my head out of respect.

"Good evening sir." I answered.

"Welcome to my pack young one."

"Thank you for taking me in, I am most grateful."

"I was told of your… situation with Vincent and I believe you have already spoke to Leanna?"

"Yes sir?"

"We are here for each other. As a pack we are strong in these troubled times. Make sure you become a useful member and you will feel the full benefits."

I nodded.

"I will take my leave as I have much to do. Some of the local villages are being ransacked. I do not like to involve myself in human matters but it's hard when our food source is being sorely depleted. I am sure I will see much more of you Ginetta."

He gave me a short nod and backed out, closing the door behind him.

I stayed in that small room for several weeks and in that time I learnt to focus. I wrote journals during the night to occupy my mind and then while I slept I dreamt of him but once I woke I thought of him no more. Leanna, as hard as she was sat with me, fascinated as I discovered my writing skill.

When I was finally ready to leave my cell I liked to think I left a piece of Vincent behind in there which enabled me to finally think that I could possibly live without him.

Damien was also very impressed with my writing skill and soon I found myself being appointed with the job of keeping records. It was a task I relished and even now I have an obsession with cataloging my life and discoveries.

The years passed and I sent a note or two back to Vincent. I slowly began to realize that the fault was neither of ours. He had not wanted me to die and I knew that even though he wanted to he could not love me as a vampire. When I had been at Damien's for five decades I decided the time had come for me to take my leave. I was not a pack animal. As grateful as I was, I wanted to be alone and I wanted to see the world.

Chapter Eleven

My wanderings over the next thousand years were uneventful. I never stayed in one place for more than a few decades and as I moved I always sent word back to Horaldo as I promised. I both loved and loathed those lonely years. My loneliness took precedence over my longing for Vincent but my heart never forgot the smell of his skin or the way his touch had set me on fire. I longed for companionship, but on the brief occasions when I found myself striking up a conversation I retreated within myself, never knowing what to say, always comparing them with Vincent. In all that time I never made love to anyone else, never had the inclination. I only craved Vincent's hands on my body. I fed only when I was hungry, out of necessity more than pleasure.

I enjoyed the ever-changing landscape of Europe and all the new inventions springing up. I had more than enough money to do as I pleased and I always indulged in the newest fashions or latest inventions and I reveled as books became more available and in so many new genres. I stayed in the most fancy of houses and lived a very lavish lifestyle. To humans I must have appeared an eccentric young woman, a loner, shut away from the world rarely venturing out.

It was in the middle of the seventeenth century that I found myself staring at a letter. It had been hand delivered and the writing on the front was familiar and sent shivers down my spine. It took me a few moments to gather myself together to open it.

Dearest Ginetta,

I can't quite believe how many years have passed. Guilt has caused me to think of you often but logic has told me to give you distance. I contact you now because I am moving to England in the next few weeks. I have bought a large plot of land, which houses an enormous underground cavern. I am currently converting it into underground quarters and I'm making plans to move there permanently. I have already acquired a following of vampires keen to settle into a pack and wanted to give you the opportunity to join me. I am hoping that the passing of years will enable you to live alongside me and aid me in what will be my biggest venture to date.

Vincent

Could I, after all this time return to him? I remembered those times we walked in the gardens before we became an item. I had so many fond memories of his company. I reasoned that he had wronged me but I knew it wasn't true, he could not help his feelings for me. I delicately laid the note down and walked to the window. I starred sadly at the star lit sky and realized I did want a purpose. I had wandered for so long, so many lonely years. I wanted to belong like I had at the villa. If I could never have love at least I could have a family.

I returned a note saying I would travel to England and contact him once I had arrived and then I set about packing my belongings. A lot of my curios were already packed in boxes. When you move every decade or so for over a thousand years you get truly fed up of it. I only repacked stuff when the boxes got so old that they disintegrated. The only thing I loved to see on display was my books. I had crate after crate of them as well as those in my library. I had my handwritten ones, and then when printing machines were invented and books flooded the market, I had been able to indulge myself. I loved to read and I read anything. I packed my books from my library lovingly away into crates to. This was to be my biggest move to date, I'd rarely ventured across the sea. Instinct makes a vampire want to be safe during the day and the thought of being on a ship, bobbing about on the open waves simply petrified me. I planned to leave the next week, with my belongings following on several weeks after and I arranged to have a house bought near to Vincent's so that I could have a few meetings with him. I was absolutely petrified that once I set eyes on him all those intense uncontrollable feelings would return, just as strong. I begged the gods for mercy, to give me the strength to live at last among others. I had never killed another being, human or vampire and I didn't take any pleasure from feeding like Horaldo or Damien.

All too soon everything I owned was packed and ready to go. I was nervous about travelling, vampires usually are. We wouldn't be long at sea but you cannot seek shelter from the sun if your ship sank.

It took three weeks for me to reach the port in France by carriage and I boarded with apprehension. The time was coming sooner; the unreachable was just out of reach. I prayed to god to ease my suffering and enable me to live some sort of life for once.

Thankfully the journey across the English Channel was short and after another week of travel I arrived at the town Vincent called home. I checked into a hotel because it was close to dawn and I wanted to be well rested before meeting him again.

I marveled at how different England was from a brief stay over five hundred years before. I hadn't stayed long because I found the people to be primitive despite the Roman influence. However as I gazed upon the elegant Ladies and Gentle in the grand Hotel I was in, I had to change my mind.

My chaperone, who had travelled the distance with me, was a human friend of Horaldo's and he guarded me for his last night in my company. He had driven the carriage so it hadn't been necessary to speak to him too much but he was a pleasant young man nonetheless and I found myself wanting to ask him to stay on, in case I changed my mind about Vincent.

At dawn I paid the chaperone handsomely, even though he was receiving a wage on his return to Horaldo. He thanked me with a deep bow, a smile and then he was gone. I was alone.

I bathed and an assistant helped me into one of my finer dresses and I ordered a carriage to take me to Vincent's address. My stomach was in butterflies.

We travelled through the bustling busy town until we reached the outskirts, where all of the wealthier businessman resided. The carriage pulled off the main road and through two huge stone pillars. The drive was winding through well-kept grounds until Vincent's mansion came into view.

It was beautiful. It looked newly built. The stone work was flawless, the windows sparkling. It was everything that I would have expected from Vincent, but in that era.

I exited, paid my fare and waited until the carriage was completely out of view, gathering my thoughts before I made my way up the immaculate steps to the huge door.

My hand reached for the knocker but froze as the door opened before my fingers made contact. A handsome young man stood in the doorway with shining brown, shoulder length hair and chiseled features.

"Miss Ginetta?"

"Yes." I answered.

"I'm Red, Vincent instructed me to see you through to the pantry. He will be arriving shortly."

"He isn't here?"

"No Miss, he had some urgent business at the cavern last night and there wasn't enough time to come home this morning."

He stepped back, inviting me in with a gracious sweep of his hand. As I passed him, I caught his scent.

"You are a vampire?"

"Yes Miss Ginetta, I have only been turned six months."

"You have good control for one so young."

"Vincent says so too, I have been able to venture out since I was a month turned. Would you like some refreshments brought to you?"

"That would be lovely."

"Bottled or fresh?"

"Bottled is preferred."

I followed him through to a beautiful room, elegantly decorated in deep red and gold wallpaper. The seating matched, the wood was gilded in gold with deep red cushioned seats. To set the room off, there were several large dark wood display cabinets with intricate carved cherub designs on them.

"If you'd like to take a seat, I shan't be long."

I perched on the far end of one of the sofas.

I couldn't smell Vincent in here, he must have chosen a room he least frequented to ease any initial suffering. Either that or it had been so long that I had forgotten his scent.

A short while later a young girl returned carrying a tray with a wine bottle and glass. She too was a vampire. She also looked nervous. New born nervous.

"Your beverage Miss Ginetta."

"Where did Red go?"

"Master Vincent just arrived and he is meeting him at the front to tell him you are here."

I took the bottle from her and removed the cork, closing my eyes and breathing in that familiar smell. The young girl began to shake a little.

"Are you okay?" I asked

"Yes, forgive me. I have only been turned a few months. This is my first week venturing round the house."

"Have you fed?"

"Yes Miss."

"You need to feed a little more. It's difficult at first, the thirst is so strong. Your first feed of the day should be great and it will ease your craving throughout the day."

"Thank you miss, I just…"

"What?" I asked softly sensing her reluctance to open up.

"I can't get used to it. I hate craving it."

"You don't have a choice my dear. Did you not want to be turned?"

"It was complicated. Red is my brother and I did not want to leave him. He has always protected me."

"Ah. Well if it's any consolation I have drank more blood from a bottle than a neck. I prefer it."

"Really?"

"Yes." I laughed at her look of disbelief.

"Most vampires prefer it fresh but if the bottled variety is available then I always opt for it."

I heard footsteps in the hall and I stood and turned.

He breezed into the room looking as handsome as ever. His hair was now long, past his shoulders. His skin was still copper toned and as my eyes met his my knees almost gave way.

"Ginetta?" He stood frozen in the doorway.

"I'm OK." I answered.

"Redvick, Elaina, you may leave and have the rest of the evening to yourselves."

"Thank you Vincent." Red answered.

The girl, Elaina, walked quickly out and gave Vincent a respectful bow on the way out. We were alone.

"You look… beautiful Gina." He breathed.

He was as dashing as ever. I remembered the last time I had been in his presence. The want the need for him was over bearing. That same need was there, no doubt, but it was manageable.

"Your hair," I whispered. "It's so long."

"I am lucky that hair is in fashion here, now."

His hair shone like spun silk and sat well below his shoulders. His eyes, the same piercing green, hooded with concern bore through to my very soul.

"It suits you."

"We have much to discuss Gina, come bring your blood and we will go to my office."

I followed and began the next part of my vampire life.

Chapter Twelve

Present day

I paced the floor. *Where the hell was he?* Red was missing, his soul mate, Robin was frantically searching for him and Vincent should have been here, ages ago.

A nasty pack had been kidnapping our members for many months and I hoped to god they hadn't gotten Red. Not one that had been captured had survived.

He had met his mate, Robin, a bold, brash model just a few weeks before and since then our well run little vampire society had erupted into chaos.

First we found out that Robin was a Santorian, an extinct breed of Vampire that died out at the time when Vincent was a newborn vampire. She was highly dangerous but Vincent had insisted on taming her against my advice I might add. We didn't have much choice though with Red being her soul mate. Next Elaina had gone missing and from evidence we gathered from her dying chaperones we deduced that this pack also had a Santorian. Oh, I forgot to mention, Santorian's drink vampire blood. They are stronger than us, faster than us and they can even go out in the sun. Vincent figured out that this pack was probably taking our members to feed their Santorian.

Vincent had also been looking for a special artifact for many years, a rare vampire ring that allows the bearer to walk in the sun. Robin had been researching with her super Santorian powers and had found a possible location. Vincent went to look for it because our best chance of finding Elaina before they drained her was to get the ring and complete Robin's training so she would be able to track these malicious kidnappers.

Vincent had gone to France, found the ring but he was late back, hours late, *too late.* Robin had just phoned asking where Red was. He had dropped me off that particular evening with more than enough time to spare to get home. I was stuck because the sun was up. My eyes were heavy telling me to sleep, but I couldn't. Robin had asked for instructions on the way Red would have drove home so she could go and look for him. She sounded frantic.

Despite my initial reservation, I'd come to love Robin dearly but she had a hell of a temper and she was a new born Santorian capable of ripping up trees and hurling them great distances. I had seen her crush rock with her bare hands. I drummed my fingers impatiently on the table next to the phone. *Where the hell were they all?*

When the phone finally rang night had fallen. I still had not heard from Vincent and the staff at Red's mansion had not seen Robin since she had left earlier during the day.

I grabbed the phone and nearly dropped it in my eagerness to answer.

"Hello!"

"Ginetta?"

"Red. Oh my god, you're ok. Thank the Gods."

"I need you to come over here right away."

"What's the matter, is it Vincent?"

"Please just come over."

He hung up the phone and I stared at it, like it would give me the answers I didn't want to hear.

I drove to Red's mansion right away; I didn't even summon human chaperones. I was surprised I wasn't stopped for speeding as several times I reached 120 mph on the country roads.

Red's mansion was in darkness as I arrived. I abandoned my car at the bottom of the stairs leaving the door open, the keys in the ignition and I rushed inside, heading straight for the elevator to take me to the basement. Red was waiting at the bottom.

"Tell me," I said as soon as stepped out.

"Come through" Red replied making his way to the basement living room. Robin was there waiting.

"Will you just fucking tell me!" I shouted.

Robin looked shocked, I had never sworn in her presence before.

"I had been taken by the enemy pack. Robin had found the location and sent Jarvis to phone Vincent. Vincent and Robin arrived at the pack base, an underground bunker but…" Red looked as if he were plucking up the courage to tell me, "It was Jarvis Ginetta, he was the one giving information to the other pack to enable them to kidnap our members. Ginetta, Jarvis murdered him."

"No!" I yelled, "Where is he? I have to see him!"

"Gina no, it's not good for you." Red ran to me and wrapped his arms around me.

"I won't believe it until I have seen him."

I was led, in trance, to the back bedroom, the smallest. The door was opened for me and there on the bed was my Vincent. My love, my only love.

I approached the bed next to him and too his hand in mine. It was still warm. Touching him sent little shock waves up and down my spine and I released I craved him still.

"Will I ever be free Vinnie?"

Red and Robin respectfully left me alone and it was at that moment, that very moment, as I held Vincent's warm dead hand in mine, that the idea came to me.

The ring, the ring that Vincent had managed to retrieve. He must have used it to get to Red in the daylight. I had done extensive research on this ring and there were two rumors about it that cropped up over and over again. Suddenly the hundreds of years reading anything I could get my hands on were worth it.

It was written that the ring gave the bearer the ability to walk in the sun. The second was that it could bring a dead vampire back to life. It was called the *Giver of Light and*

Life. If the first were true then what if the second was too. What if I could save him?

I left Vincent slowly. There was no time to lose. His body would decay very slowly but I had no idea of my window of opportunity, if it even existed at all. I just knew above anything that my heart would not let him die if there was a miniscule opportunity that I could breathe life into him once more.

"Don't worry Gina. We'll take care of everything." Red said softly as I returned to the sitting room.

"No." I said quickly. "I want to do it. I don't want to burn him, I want to place him in a mausoleum."

"We can't do that, it's not how it's done," Red protested.

"It's how it's going to be done this time! I'm not ready, don't you understand? I can't stand the thought of burning him!" I had no intention of telling them about the plan forming in my head. It was ludicrous and even I knew how slim a chance it was that it would actually be possible. I changed the subject

I could see that robin looked tired. I wanted to hear the full story of how my beloved came to his end and she was the best one to tell me.

"Let's have a seat and I'll feed you." I said to her.

I was shocked at how Vincent had met his end and it made me even more determined to see if I could resurrect him. It wasn't quite as straightforward as that, though. I was Vincent's second in command and I had inherited a huge vampire pack to run. I gave Red, Robin, Elaina, who had been rescued from the pack in time and the pack's Santorian, Ethan who turned out to be Elaina's soul mate a few weeks off to recover from the whole ordeal. I direly needed the help but I needed to do lots of research and I didn't want anyone questioning me.

One of my jobs as Vincent's right hand lady had been to archive all our research onto the computer and it was all stored on handy pen drives. I pulled up everything about the artifact I could lay my hands on that gave reference to it being 'the giver of light and life'. I printed everything out and shut myself up in my bedroom and began to read.

Most articles were diaries and references to people that had owned the artifact. Many had been dismissed because they had not revealed a location for us. One scripture we had dismissed caught my eye.

It spoke of the vampire who had mined the stones and discovered their special properties. Vincent had dismissed this article because the vampire in question lived in deep isolation in the mountains of Tibet. He was called Kilvire and he was rumored to be 30,000 years old. He was dangerous to all who approached him; in fact, no one had any reference to meeting him in the last thousand years.

I was going to Tibet.

I sent Red and Robin to Italy to meet with Horaldo, who was now running a pack there. Horaldo had heard about the great battle in the bunker and he was eager to meet our Santorian. I received news that the meeting had gone incredibly well and Red had actually found his mother who was a vampire in Horaldo's pack. They asked if they could stay on and I happily gave permission. It gave me the perfect cover to go to Tibet to try to find Kilvire.

Even though I was in charge I could not ask anyone could to accompany me because they would ask questions.

I flew first class on my own, fool hardy, yes. It was a long flight and I took it not even planning if I would be covered once I arrived.

Luckily it was night when we landed and I sought out the hotel I'd booked into, The Midnight Sunrise. It was special because it was run by vampires, for vampires. I'd booked the best, most expensive room so I was greeted specially by the owner himself.

"Good evening Miss. I have your room ready, although you have plenty of time before sunrise. My name is Lance, you may contact me night or day if you need anything."

"Thank you."

Lance was not your average, good-looking vampire. He was tall, thin, very pale and almost white blond. He also sounded Swedish.

He led me through to my suite of rooms and opened the door with the key card before handing it to.

"There is one thing I need lance, before tomorrow night if it's possible."

"Yes Miss, anything."

"I need to know the last location of Kilvire and I also need people that will take me there."

Lance looked caught between surprise, shock and anger.

"Out of the question Miss."

"I will pay handsomely, money is no object." Having anticipated reluctance to hand over information I pulled a think wad of one hundred pound notes from my handbag. Lance practically drooled.

"Now listen. I just need the location, people to get me there, food to sustain me and I need to be brought back. No one needs to be put into danger, that will be for myself alone."

"Well…"

"This money is for you, organize me the people. I will pay anyone who help me separately, this money is yours alone and I will give you double the amount on my return."

"I will see what I can do." His eyes didn't leave the wad of money the whole time we spoke.

True to his word, the following night Lance met me in the foyer. He had with him three Vampires and four humans.

"These vampires will take you to the last known location and the humans will guard you during the day. It will take you three days on horseback to get there and one full day on foot."

"Thank you Lance."

"You are a fool Miss."

"I beg your pardon."

"Many before you have sought him out. The need for his wisdom, but you will only find death and disappointment. He is rumored to have gone mad."

"It matters not, I must seek him out."

He gave me a curt nod and left.

The eight of us saddled up and began our journey. We each had a horse of our own and we had three extra horses carrying provisions and such.

We quickly left the busy town behind and were soon in unpopulated terrain. The mountains could be seen in the distance looming over us, mocking me to my doom. We let the horses rest half way through the first night and made small idle chitchat. I was happy to sit on the sidelines and watch the group chatter on eager to be back on our journey.

As the sun began to lighten we stopped once more and the four humans erected a large tent. The material was thick and the tents had four outer layers preventing any sunlight coming through. I bedded down and listened to the humans outside taking turns two at a time guarding while the other two slept. I didn't feel the cold, I was capable of it but I was numb to all senses. I was solely focused on my goal even though a part of me knew I was not likely to survive.

The following two nights were the same. On the forth night we abandoned the humans and horses to make the final part of the journey on foot. We were deep into the mountains with no path to follow. I wanted to ask how my comrades could possibly know where to go. One had a compass but neither of the three had a map.

We began to climb. Luckily we made short work of the first part of the mountain and then one of the vampires pointed to a path, old an overgrown.

"There. You follow to the other side."

"Where will you wait?"

"We will wait here until dawn. If you have not returned we will stay, though for one day only."

"OK."

Without another word I turned and left. The path was traitorous. The drop to my left was several hundred feet and in places the path that hugged the side of the mountain had crumbled away to merely a foot across. Some steps I took sent little stones falling down the side of the mountain making me gasp and question what the hell I was really doing.

The path led me round to a natural archway in the mountain. It became wider and easier to navigate. As I rounded a corner I gasped as a temple came into view.

It was small, set into the mountain and accessible via a long winding set of thin dangerous looking stone stairs.

I had found it. I only hope Kilvire survived still.

I carefully made my way to the top of the stairs and stood outside the temples huge peeling red doors. Should I knock? Should I just go in?

I knocked. The sound reverberated around the mountain and I could hear it echo from within the temple itself.

No one answered so I tried the door. I lifted the heavy iron latch and it swung inwards. Inside was a huge barren room with pillars the width of tree trunks holding the mighty roof in place. There were no seats just a stone floor beneath my feet and an altar at the far end. A second glance told me I was not alone.

A man sat on the altar table. He was looking straight at me. I gulped and made my way down the middle of the temple and approached him.

His eyes were black, the whole of his eyes, even the whites. He was bald but well built. He also looked as if he might strike out at any moment. He was specular. His skin was the palest I had seen on a vampire but it only enhanced his presence. He wore a slight smile on his chiseled, devilishly sculpted face, a look not unlike a cat before it starts playing with the little mouse it's caught for dinner. I was petrified.

"Kilvire?" I whispered

"What makes you think I will even give you what you seek Ginetta the Roman?"

I was momentarily stunned.

He laughed softly in response.

"I could read your mind from the time you entered the town. You have thought of nothing else. *Does the ring work? Can I save him?* Questions, Questions Ginetta of Rome."

His voice was sinister and my heart sank. I had the worst feeling in the world.

"I won't be killing you just yet Ginetta. I am curious. I have not had one approach me with such selfless need before. You would go to this length, for a vampire who cannot love you in return?"

"Yes Sir."

"Lance was right, you are a fool." He saw my puzzled expression. "I don't know him but I can read his thoughts. I can read the thoughts of any human or vampire within one hundred miles of this temple."

"Please, can you help me?" I asked simply

"I'm not sure yet. Not sure I even want to."

I hung my head. He laughed once more

"Love is a powerful thing Ginetta of Rome."

"Have you ever…"

"Yes I have found my soul mate, twice in fact. I killed them." He said bluntly.

I was horrified.

"I won't have anyone have power over me that I can't control."

He really was mad.

"Not mad, just an old vampire, set in his ways."

I tried not to think about anything, but it was impossible. I thought how stupid I had been in covering my tracks so carefully. No one would know I'd come to Tibet if I died. I was glad I hadn't brought the ring with me.

"Ah my ring, you found it."

"Yes sir."

"And now you want to know how it works."

"Yes." I whispered.

"Have you used it in the day. How was it?"

"Magnificent, I had forgotten how wonderful it was."

"To feel the sun on your face is wonderful." He raised his hand, the full scarlet robes covering his hand and arm slipped down revealing an identical ring. "Would you still want the secret if I told you that you had to give that up. This ring and the one in your possession are the only ones left in existence. Ask yourself Ginetta of Rome is he worth giving up such a precious gift?"

"Yes." I said without hesitation.

He stopped. He craned his neck slightly. This was the first movement he had made since I had arrived; he slowly covered his arm and placed them both in his lap.

"Sit." He commanded. I sat without question on the stone floor at his feet. "I can see your thoughts and I know that you are truthful.

I will tell you the secret Ginetta. The prize is fine but the cost is hard and may even kill you in the process."

"I am ready." I said in earnest.

"Listen carefully then you may leave to get back to your group before dawn.

The ring has five Embala stones in it. The Embala stones are the source of the power and you will need four of them. You must first repair the damage to Vincent's heart. Then you must place a stone in each of the chambers of the heart and seal him back up. Then you must feed him from the same vampire each night until he wakens, it is important, in your particular situation that this vampire be you. If you are successful, you will know why. If he does not get enough of your blood he will not come back. If you give him too much then you will die. The only hint that you will have it is working is his heart will start to shudder a few days before he wakes, when you hear this give as much blood as you are able. The blood must be taken from you and administered directly into the heart. Still going ahead."

I would be lying if I said I wasn't scared at my task but it hadn't deterred me.

"I thought so. Leave now, Ginetta of Rome, and warn the others that seeking me out again is not a good idea. I will not be so accommodating to my next visitors."

"Thank you." I stood and bowed my head in respect.

I had managed to complete the first part of my mission in a few days and I touched down in Manchester ready to complete the next part but not quite sure if I was capable of doing so.

I held a meeting to get up to speed about the packs business. Everything was ticking over nicely. Vincent had run a meticulously tight ship and it showed. Once I was sure that everything was running smoothly I headed to the local bookshop, caught it just before closing and purchased a large amount of medical text books.

My first port of call was to learn a little about open-heart surgery. I headed to my apartment within the depths of the cavern, got a bottle of the finest and sat at the huge table in my dining room with the ridiculously oversized books.

Half way through the next day my brain was fried but I could safely say I knew the ins and outs of the human heart as well as any surgeon. The only trouble now was I had to go and open up the only person I ever loved and repairs something that might in fact is irreparable.

I decided to get some rest and try not to think about the gruesome task I had to do next.

The next night I rested till well after midnight. I wanted to perform the surgery during the day. I would be well sheltered from the sun within the Mausoleum and there were be no risk of anyone looking for me.

Luckily we had all the necessary things I would need, as our medical bay was more than well equipped for emergencies of any sort.

I took a large bag, headed down to the heart of the cavern and loaded up everything I would need.

I checked in with our managers who oversaw various areas of the pack and tied up loose ends before people started to retire for the day.

I retrieved my bag and headed outside.

The cavern was based underneath an old church. It had been used during ancient wars as a hideout and then Vincent had purchased it in the sixteenth century and had begun carving it out.

I had watched it grow literally from a cave to an underground vampire city with running water, electricity and gas. About five hundred vampires resided within its walls. The more prominent like myself had apartments that apart from the lack of windows wouldn't have been out of place in a swanky block of flats.

In the grounds of the church above sat an old crumbling cemetery that hadn't been used for hundreds of years. It was here I had created an elaborate mausoleum for Vincent. It was made from the finest grey granite and was secured with a thick iron gate and the metal door had a code entry system, I was the only one that knew the key.

I unlocked the gate, coded in the key and swung open the thick steel door. My beloved was led, as he had been the day we placed him there on a stone altar, in the center of the room.

I had dressed him in his finest tailored suit and brushed his hair till it shone like spun gold and rested on the polished stone beneath him.

His skin had not lost its bronze color and his lips had only just started to dull to a purplish red. I closed the door behind me, approached him and kissed him lightly on the forehead. I felt that familiar jolt up my spine and I closed my eyes savoring the love that flowed through my veins.

"Forgive me my love, though it is torture that you can never love me, I cannot live without you."

I eased his suit off him and unbuttoned his shirt exposing his chest. I ran my fingers over the wound at his heart. He had been staked from behind so the wound was only an inch hole and didn't look too bad. I tilted my head and thought the wound looked low down. I reckoned it had hit the lower part of the heart. Well it was time for find out for sure.

I retrieved a scalpel and rib separators. I did not have to worry about blood flow obviously but I got out gauze and such to mop up any blood that might be left within him.

I ran the scalpel down his chest from the base of his neck to a few inches below his rib cage.

The flesh opened and I continued, carefully along the same line until I met bone. I could smell his blood, fueling a fire within me, spurring me on in my task. Next I peeled away the layer of skin and muscle covering the left side of his ribs. I glanced up, half expecting Vincent to be looking back at me but he lay in his eternal slumber.

I gulped as I finally had reached the part of this I had been dreading.

From my bag I took a small circular saw, sinister and deadly looking. I switched it on. It whirled into life, sounding a little like a dentist's drill. I prayed I could complete the task before the batteries ran out.

I carefully, make that, very carefully touched the edge of the spinning blade to the top of his sternum and it cut through the bone as if it were butter. I carried on and carefully cut a square shape then lifted it off exposing the heart.

It was strange seeing it there, not beating. The wound was as I thought; it has penetrated the lower end of the heart damaging only one chamber. I was very lucky. I wiped the area clean and carefully lifted the heart so I could see the back. I breathed the biggest sigh of relief. I had set myself up to repair a pulverized heart but I could see that it would be much simpler, well as simple as open heart surgery on a vampire could be.

I next got needles and fine stitches and repaired the tear on the chamber in the back. Then using clamps I sealed the outside and stitched that too. It looked neat. From my pocket I produced a small suede pouch and I gently tipped the contents onto the altar. The five stones I had picked from the ring lay sparkling up at me. Using a pair of tweezers I picked up the first stone carefully and placed it into the wound and deep in the first chamber of his heart.

Then using the same method as I had on his back I stitched up the front. I held the organ in one hand, touched it lightly almost caressing it, willing my stupid plan to work then I gently replaced it back in the ribcage. Now I had to get the other stones into the three remaining chambers. Next

I retrieved a long thick steel needle and inserted it into the upper chamber, above the wound. Satisfied I had the needle inserted in the right place I picked up another tiny stone, popped it in the end of the needle, and then I used a thin skewer type rod to make sure the stone had hit home. I repeated the process on the final two chambers at the other side then I took a well-deserved break and took a bottle of blood from my bag.

I chugged it back until I felt so full I might burst. I never gorged on blood, only ever took as much as I needed to live but this was a different case, I needed to be at maximum strength.

I replaced the square section of the sternum, eased the skin back over and sewed up the wound. Kilvire had stated that blood needed to be pumped directly into the heart. I decided the best way would be to insert the same metal needle into the main vein at the top of the heart itself. I then planned on leaving it in place so I could feed my blood directly in at each session.

After the needle was in place I took out a catheter and tourniquet and found a vein in my own arm. I then started to withdraw my own blood into a waiting blood bag. This was easier said than done. Our blood is far thicker than human blood; it almost has the consistency of syrup. I filled one bag and began on another. About half way through I began to feel woozy. I stupidly kept going until I passed out.

I came to on the stone floor of the altar, momentarily wondering where the hell I was and wondering if I had dreamed the whole charade.

The tubes in my arm and the bag attached to the end of it told me to get the hell up and carry on. I struggled to my feet, attached the first bag of blood to the needle and watched as it very slowly began to filter through.

It was noon and I was tired. My body naturally wanted to sleep when the sun was high and I was fighting with everything I had to stay awake. When the first bag was empty I held up the second one until it too was empty. I made a mental note to bring a drip stand.

I still had a few hours until sundown so I cleared away my equipment, climbed on to the altar and fell asleep nestled in the crook of Vincent's arm.

My watch told me night had fallen. I felt groggy and still tired. I wanted to lie back down and sleep once more but people would wonder where I was and besides I needed to replenish my blood.

Red and Robin were waiting in the living room. I had totally forgotten they were due in. I wasn't in the mood for catch up.

"Hi Gina… Holy crap, you look like shit!"

"Thanks for the observation Robin. I just haven't fed yet is all." I picked up the phone on a side table and dialed through to my human assistant. "Bring a bottle please, make it two"

"How long since you fed?" Robin wasn't giving in. I felt guilty because she genuinely looked worried. Robin only worried about people she cared about. She had this go to hell attitude and I loved her dearly for it, just not right then.

"It's been a rough couple of days, it's a lot to take on, the pack. I've been busy."

I took a seat in an armchair and Red and Robin sat opposite on the sofa. Red looked equally concerned.

"Ginetta, we would not have stayed in Rome had we known you were struggling. Where did you sleep? "

"Conference room" I answered quickly.

"Oh really?" Robin asked looking at me like she knew I was lying.

"It's not healthy visiting him, he's dead. We loved him but he should have been cremated Gina…"

"I don't want to talk about it." I snapped

Robin came and sat on the arm of the sofa and placed a hand on my shoulder.

"It's fine, I'm sorry. You do what you have to do to get through this OK. We are here now. We can move into the cavern, help you run things."

"No, its fine. Let's let things tick over as they were before. You guys stay at home and report nightly. Now you're here, if I need help, I will ask for it."

"Are you sure?" Red asked

"Yes, now come on, fill me in on everything that has happened."

It took all my energy to stay awake and listen to the full story of them meeting Horaldo and then discovering that Red's mother, Ilona was still alive. Red was really happy and Robin seemed to have warmed to her as well. Ilona and her soul mate, Redvick, (Red was actually named after him), were due to visit. It would be Ilona's first visit to Britain since becoming a vampire.

When the sky was tingling with the first sign of sunrise I made my way back to Vincent, this time with a drip stand. I forced down half a bottle of blood, still feeling full from the bottle I had drank in Red and Robin's company.

I only managed to fill one bag before I passed out. Once I had come to I hooked Vincent up to the drip and lay on the altar once more and slept.

I awoke several hours later, stiff and uncomfortable and forced down the other half of the bottle of blood. I loosened the knots in my shoulders and lower back and then lay down once more. The last thing I remember looking at was the bag, hanging on the drip, empty.

Over the next two weeks I became the master of disguise. I even wore make-up. This is a simple concept for most people but I, being a two thousand and odd year old vampire had never worn it, it barely existed when I'd been human. Now all of a sudden I was bombarded with concealers, tinted moisturizers, mineral foundation, hundreds of products and I didn't have the first clue. I chose what I deemed to be the basics. A stick to color over my dark circles, a liquid to give my face some color and I left it at that.

I think Red and Robin knew I spent a lot of time with Vincent, but it was never brought up again, never mentioned. I had started checking Vincent's heart with a stethoscope for any faint sign of life but nothing.

I was disheartened. The blood was going into him. I had pumped pints of it into his heart it was going somewhere, surely.

Ilona and her soul mate arrived and I gave Red and Robin time off to show them the sights and then suggested a meeting in a week just to introduce the pack base. I didn't see the point in inviting them to the cavern; they had come on holiday to see Red and Robin. It was pleasure not business.

Just as I was giving up hope, wondering why the hell I was draining myself night after night the curling up in the arms of a dead man I heard it. I was led on the altar drifting off to sleep. The stethoscope was in my ears and my hand was laid on his chest holding the other end in place.

Glug

It was so faint and I was on the cusp of sleep that I dismissed it. My heart picked up a beat anyway.

Glug

I heard it that time. I waited, counting the seconds. Forty passed

Glug.

I nearly squealed. I kissed him on the forehead.

"Come back to me…" I whispered softly in his ear.

The next few days were astounding. It was like watching a seed you had planted grow. The wound in his chest had begun to heal, as had the scar from my DIY surgery. I drank blood at every opportunity and against my better nature even fed from humans we had for that purpose within the cavern. I gave as much blood as I possibly could. Passing out each time and even squeezing out another few milliliters afterward.

Soon his wounds had healed completely yet he showed no signs of life apart from the slow glug from his heart every minute or so. I was by no means through the woods yet.

Chapter Thirteen

"Are you kidding me?" I said in disbelief down the phone to Red the next evening.

"Nope, I'm afraid not." He replied

"So you are telling me that this woman, Katrina made Redvick?"

"Yes."

"And then, against Ilona's will Katrina turned her when she dying."

"From childbirth, yes."

"And for turning her without permission, Horaldo punished her."

"Yup."

"And this was when Red was how old?"

"Four, I think."

"And this Katrina told Horaldo and Ilona that Red was OK, when he wasn't?"

"Yes, he'd actually been abandoned in an orphanage."

"Wow, so how did it get from that to Robin killed her an hour ago!" I was tired but in sheer puzzlement at what I was being told.

"Katrina had returned to England and Ilona looked her up when she arrived, to find out why she had lied about Red, we actually found out it was Katrina who introduced Vincent to Red, encouraging him to turn him."

"That's terrible. So all that time Ilona thought her son had grown up and died?"

"Yes, Ilona wanted answers but when she arrived Katrina tried to kill her."

"My god!"

"Not just kill her, she broke Ilona's leg and started slicing her up with a scalpel. She is a mess"

"The poor thing. Do you have enough reserves for her to heal?"

"We do but something else has come to light."

"There's more?"

"Her transition was traumatic, the worse I've heard of, she lay unconscious for the first ten years of her vampire life."

"Really!"

"Yes, Redvick was dedicated, feeding her when others said to put her out of her misery. The thing is when she awoke she had lost her vampire strength. She is more like a human in that way."

"You mean she can't quickly regenerate."

"No, we don't even know if her leg will heal."

"And Robin, how is she?"

"Pissed off mostly, Katrina staked her."

"Oooh… she hates that."

"Anyway, Redvick has told Horaldo and he is coming right away for a full investigation. More of a formality as it is obvious that it was self-defense."

"When will he be here?"

"Tomorrow."

"I will schedule a meeting."

I hung up the phone in despair. Could someone maybe not get murdered, or staked or sliced up just for a few weeks, just so I could see if my foolhardy plan would work.

I began drinking blood straight away. If I was to feed Vincent and have a meeting with Horaldo I needed to be on the ball. I was actually looking forward to seeing him once more it had been a few centuries. I was happy he was running his own pack.

I did my nightly duties, opened my mail, made necessary phone calls to some business's and made a point to drink at least a glass of blood every hour.

I took a bottle down with me to the mausoleum and as I extracted the blood from my arm I chugged it down straight from the wine bottle in my other.

I listened to the faint beat of his heart, willing his eyes to twitch; anything but he was totally unresponsive. At dusk with a heavy heart and a heaving head I made my way back to the cavern for the meeting.

I stopped by my apartment and sat for a few moments. I had a little time until the meeting was scheduled to start. I just wanted to close my eyes for a few minutes…

When I awoke I realized I was ten minutes late. I made my way to the conference room. I felt particularly dizzy and disoriented and several times had to stop and try to get a grip on myself.

"Gina in the name of God what has happened to you!" Red spoke as I entered the room, Robin rushed to my side to help me sit

"I'm fine, just thirsty." I replied.

One of our well respected pack members, Malachi stood and laid a hand on my shoulder.

"I will go and get you some nourishment."

I tried to focus and I turned to Horaldo.

"Horaldo, how lovely to see you again. Please excuse me I sometimes go a little too long in between feeds, my workload gets on top of me sometimes."

"Don't be sorry my dear, this pack is larger than my own and I have a time keeping tabs on everything. If I can assist you while I'm here then tell me."

"Gina," Robin said sounding very hurt. "You should have told us that you needed help, we could share more of the workload."

"It's fine honestly, don't fret. I'll feed and I'll be fine."

Malachi returned with a large wine glass of blood. I drank it in a few gulps, ignoring the eyes fixed upon me. I felt my energy levels rise slightly.

"Well, perhaps you would like to recount the evening in question Ilona." Horaldo asked.

Horaldo seemed most impressed with Robin who had taken a seat at my side and not removed her hand from my lap. Ilona recounted the same tale that Red had told me over the phone. Red's mother looked to be a fragile thing. I could barely hear her when she spoke. Horaldo seemed most impressed with Robin who had taken a seat at my side and not removed her hand from my lap.

"Astounding, I would have loved to have seen you in action my dear."

"I am truly sorry I killed her, but I really do despise being staked."

"Well I can understand that. I can see that it was not a decision you took lightly after all you walked away leaving her unharmed, she retaliated. I should have left her out in the sun to fry when she turned Ilona. My instincts told me to do so. It nearly cost you your vampire life, Ilona."

"Its fine, Robin really came through for me."

"Indeed we are in your debt, Robin."

"Don't mention it," Robin replied. "What are alliances for, huh." she grinned.

Chatter broke out and I was happy to observe, drifting in and out of listening.

"We have room back at the mansion," Robin addressed Horaldo, "You are more than welcome to stay with us."

"Why thank you that is most…"

Horaldo was cut off by the door to the conference room as it was thrown open.

Vincent stood in the doorway.

"Vincent…" Red rushed to him. "Impossible"

Vincent braced himself on the doorframe for support. His eyes locked with mine. He knew, knew it was I who had resurrected him.

"How is this possible?" Red gently touched Vincent's shoulder.

"I need, blood, please." He gasped

Robin grabbed my empty glass and topped it quickly with a bottle Malachi had brought back.

"How? Someone please tell me?" Red asked.

"It was me," I answered "I brought him back to life."

A few moments of silence broken only by the sound of Vincent gulping his blood like a newborn.

"A ring of prophecy, you found a ring of prophecy." It was Horaldo that broke the silence.

"Yes," I said, "A giver of light and life."

"You must tell me how, I have heard rumors but I did not know it was possible. You must tell me."

"I will Horaldo but please will you allow us a night to recover. The process has taken more out of me than I thought and I want to tell you everything."

Vincent approached me slowly, still very weak.

"I can't believe what you have done for me Ginetta, my love." He looked at me intensely. "Something has shifted, I feel different."

"You will my love." I told him "You died"

"No, I mean towards you. I want you. I want your touch. I crave it even though I feel I cannot even stand."

"What do you mean Vincent?"

"I don't know, but surely it is impossible. It seems as if the process has bound us."

It clicked; Kilvire's words echoed in my head, him telling me I had to be the one to bring Vincent back. I didn't have time to contemplate his words before he launched himself on me, almost knocking me over. His lips met mine and he kissed me urgently, feverishly

"Uh-hum" Horaldo cleared his throat. "Perhaps we should retire and meet up tomorrow."

Vincent stopped our kiss, still looking puzzled.

"I'm sorry. I too am confused and disorientated. Perhaps it's a good idea. I don't even know what date it is."

"My old friend," Horaldo said, rising and patting him on the back. "I assure you we are all very, very confused, but we shall wait until tomorrow."

Without replying Vincent began kissing me once more. His hands roamed my back and buttocks squeezing and kneading my flesh. I didn't even hear the door shut as everyone left.

Chapter Fourteen

Vincent chuckled then in the next moment looked at me, and a small tear formed in the corner of his eye. I reached up and wiped it away with my thumb.

"My love" I whispered, "Why do you cry?"

He brought me into a fierce embrace and whispered in my ear.

"It feels like every cell, every part of me hungers for you, like I might die if I can't touch you."

I laughed softly.

"I am here Vincent, always, I'm yours"

"That is the torment, for two thousand years you have felt like this. I thought about you all the time, but more from my own guilt than truly understanding how you felt. Gina, my poor Gina."

"Vincent, it was no more your fault than it was mine. If I could have the option of never running into you on that cobbled street two thousand years ago. If I had the option to live out the life of a normal human being, I wouldn't change it Vincent. I loved you as a human and I have waited all this time, hoping, praying that one day, I could be yours once more."

He answered by closing his mouth over mine and kissing me softly. A kiss that reminded me of our very first kiss, where I had given my innocence to him. Without breaking away he lifted me and smiled, interrupting what I would have been happy to carry on doing all night.

"Where?" He said hoarsely

"My apartment," I replied. "Put me down, I can walk, you are still weak."

"And you my love are light as a feather."

He carried me slowly through the passageways to my apartment. We passed several pack members who passed, smiled, did a huge double take, then bowed and muttered apologies for not recognizing Vincent.

Vincent didn't answer, didn't even acknowledge them. He was using every ounce of strength he had left to get us to our goal.

When we reached my apartment door I reached and opened the handle, Vincent then kicked it open and shouldered it shut behind us. He took us straight through to my bedroom, set me down and began yanking my clothes off.

"Vincent" I laughed.

He continued, only stopping to kiss me or nuzzle into my neck. When I had the opportunity I began to work the buttons on his shirt. Feelings I had learnt to bury deep inside me began coming to the surface as my fingers made contact with his chest as I awkwardly fiddled the buttons open.

When his chest was bare I ran my fingers lightly over the flesh I had carved out, not quite believing it had worked.

The skin was now smooth with no evidence of what now lay within his slow beating heart.

Suddenly I was overwhelmed. He was back. He was here and we were bonded.

I threw my arms around him. My naked chest made contact with his stomach and we both felt the sexual tension increase.

Vincent grunted a reply, eased me back on the bed and in a flash, relived himself of his trousers.

There was no foreplay, Vincent began kissing me once more, parted my legs and entered me to his hilt.

"Holy fuck!" He said loudly. "Ginetta, my sweet Gina."

"Don't stop Vincent."

He obliged me but much to his disappoint released himself a couple of minutes later.

"Oh my god, I don't believe, I've never come that quickly since… I've never come that quickly!"

I chuckled and snuggled in. After a few moments I rose, padded through to my kitchen and returned quickly with some blood. My fridge was always stocked well.

I swirled the blood round within the bottle because it tends to start to separate after a few hours, then I handed Vincent a glass and filled it to the top.

"I honestly don't know how you manage to stomach this Gina." He said taking a sip.

"We all have our tastes, you usually have several" I winked at him.

"I feel bad now," he said hanging his head

"Why!"

"You've been here for three hundred years, watching me with other women. I'm a monster."

"Vincent honestly, I didn't have to stay did I but I wanted to."

"Ok, answer me something?"

"Yes."

"Please, please, for the love of the gods tell me that you did not seek out Kilvire?"

I didn't answer.

"Gina, you fool!"

He was angry now.

"I'm fine, look, it worked."

"It's not the point…" he was suddenly distracted "How?"

"Do you really want to know?"

"Of course I do."

I proceeded to tell him.

Ten minutes later Vincent had visibly paled.

"I actually think I may throw up"

"Oh come on! You are a warrior."

"You performed open heart surgery, I mean, how did even know where to start?"

"Book, lots of books, no, *LOADS* of books."

He looked down and ran his fingers over the smooth flesh on his sternum.

"And they are in there? Now?"

"Yes."

"It's hard to imagine."

"I know, but you are here. The ring will not work now, there's only one stone left."

"I can hardly complain."

Vincent thought for a few moments.

"How long was I dead?"

"Weeks, just weeks"

"And the one who killed me?"

"It was Jarvis?"

"Jarvis! Please Gina, you must tell me all that has happened."

It was hard to know where to start; so much had happened in the short time he had been gone. There was the fact the fact that the Santorian of the enemy pack that was responsible for killing Vincent, now resided with us and was Red's sister's soul mate. His name was Ethan and once his bloodlust had been tamed we found him to be a quietly spoken man who was besotted with Elaina.

Then the big whammy was the fact that Red's Mom, Ilona was alive (undead) and well and had been a member of Horaldo's group all this time. I barely had details to give him because I could hardly remember the previous weeks due to the fact that I had been drained to within an inch of my life.

He badgered me and badgered me for details I couldn't give then finally gave in so we could sleep. We were both exhausted.

I awoke to someone nuzzling my hair and growling in my ear. My body responded before I was fully awake.

Vincent's hand came from behind me, cupping my breast and teasing the nipple. Little shivers ran up and down my spine and I arched my back and moaned softly.

Vincent guided himself inside me and bit into my neck. He drew only a little blood and pumped in and out of me in great long slow strokes. He gripped my hip so he could enter me as fully as possible. It was delicious. I could feel every part of him caressing my insides. He drew lazily from my vein, stopping to lick the thin trail running down my neck and then latching on once more.

I snaked my hand round to feel his taunt bare buttocks working at a pace behind me. He quickened his strokes then gasped as he came.

"Morning." I said collapsed into the bed behind me.

"Mmm, I don't know which is worse my hunger or my lust for you, woman"

"I'll go get you something to eat."

"Make it fresh, no bottled stuff."

"I think Malachi had a couple of ladies at his apartment would you like one."

"God yes, send two."

I chuckled.

"I'll go feed myself and I'll give you a couple of hours."

"Hours, why would I need hours?"

"Erm, well you know to feed and erm…"

"Ye gods Gina, they'll be none of that now. Malachi can deal with them after. Don't leave me, I want to hold you some more."

My heart pounded at his words. I had so longed for Vincent to want me and only me. That dream had been snatched away with Carlina's bitter betrayal. I Leaned over and kissed him gently, softly. He closed his eyes.

"It feels so strange how a kiss, just a kiss can be so… intense."

"I know, my love. You will adjust."

I made my way to Malachi's underground apartment. He didn't always stay underground as he ran a huge office complex for the pack and had a special underground apartment there. He had two girls that stayed at the cavern if he needed. He had also been seeing a lot of Robin's house manager Danni, a lovely ex-model human.

I knocked on the door and was surprised when Malachi himself answered.

"Ginetta, thank god."

"Is everything OK?"

"Well yes, after we left there was a delivery for you."

"For me, here?"

"Yes, come in."

His apartment was masculine and modern; most of his furnishings were dark wood and black leather. He also had dark wood floors as well as modern art scaling the walls.

He left and returned carrying a heavy old fashioned enveloped with a wax seal on the front. Puzzled I popped open the seal and my eyes adjusted to the ancient scrawled writing

Ginetta of Rome

I require your presence once more. I hope your 'experiment' went well. Come right away, it is a matter of urgency.

Kilvire.

"Holy crap!" I said. "I need to tell Vinnie."

"What is it?"

"No time, schedule a meeting in two hours please."

"Who is to be in attendance?"

"Robin, Red, Horaldo… just everyone that was here yesterday. Explanations are needed. Can you spare some girls for Vinnie?"

"Sure, Danni stayed the night so I can spare them both."

"Send them over to my apartment and I'll see you in two hours"

Crap, crap, crap, I thought as I made my way to the blood storage room. What did Kilvire want? I couldn't not go. After all, he had given me the information I had sought and he had let me live. Vincent was going to go mad. He knew more about Kilvire than anyone, knew the horrible things he had done. He was a vampire that firmly believed that humans were cattle. He did not discriminate against sex, age or race. He was a plague but if I didn't go god knows what he might do. I grabbed a bottle and headed back taking my time so that Vincent could feed.

"I'm going with you."

I'd returned after I'd fed to find Vincent waiting for me looking considerably better. I'd shown him the letter.

"No!" I said panicking; I didn't want to put him in danger.

"It's not even up for discussion"

"But what if…"

"I don't care. I can't believe you approached him in the first place."

"I'm glad I did." I said hanging my head.

He was there in an instant, holding me. He smoothed my hair.

"I'm sorry, it's just I met him once, when I was very young it was…"

He shuddered.

"I would have battled him to get you back."

"I know, I know that now."

"I've asked for everyone to meet, to explain everything."

"When?"

"Just over an hour from now"

"We have time," he smiled, "I ran us a bath."

"Lovely." I breathed.

I am a simple creature, as times changed and new things were invented I was sometimes stuck in my ways. I didn't need the latest sound system installed the second it was released and I didn't need a big luxurious apartment like Vinnie's or Malachi's. One thing I did enjoy was a bath. When Vincent had had running water installed I installed a large square bath with a Jacuzzi and headrests. I liked to fill it up to the top and lie in it until it became tepid. It took me back to my first bath with Anazia. I smiled at the thought of when we had kissed.

Vincent had filled the bath to nearly full and had added my favorite bubble bath. He had acquired some black jeans but wore nothing else. He really was spectacular, just to look at him you could imagine him in battle. He had been bred by vampires to be a fighter, and it showed. There wasn't an ounce of fat on him. The muscles of his stomach were clearly defined and the ones over his hips dip down to a crisp bed of light sandy hair. I had never seen him naked since ancient Rome. He was timeless, was exactly as I remembered. His hair was like silk, sitting softly passed his shoulders and his skin, unlike most vampires was a dark olive. He got down on his knees and laid his head on my stomach.

"I love you Gina."

I ran my fingers in his hair.

"And I you, Vincent."

He planted small kisses on my stomach. I motioned to kneel down and join him but he grasped my knee, holding it up, pressed his mouth to me intimately and began to devour me. I let my head drop back as he worked me with his tongue and fingers. The sensations were far more intense than when I been human. We were tuned into one another, joined, bonded. We had made love twice in such a short amount of time Vincent had been back but this was far more intense. Using his spare hand he slid two fingers inside me, exploring, teasing, nibbling all at the same time. I felt an orgasm building inside me but it was overwhelming, on the verge of being painful. I grasped his hair tightly urging him to stop, wanting him to continue.

I cried out loudly gripping his hair tightly as I had my first orgasm as a vampire. It ripped through me bringing heat to my chest and making me cry out.

Vincent rested his head on my stomach once more.

"You even taste different, like a drug."

I knelt down and joined him.

"I'm surprised you can remember what I taste like."

"You always were my favorite."

"I know." I smiled.

"I wish…" He trailed off.

"Hey," I said sternly, "There's no point in wishing things could've been different because they couldn't have been. You couldn't force yourself to love me no more than you can stop loving now."

"It'd hurts to think about what I've put you through."

"We need to move on, together"

"I know, I'll try, I've only been reborn a few hours, give me a chance."

"Vincent, I have always known that love would find a way. I learnt how to bury my feelings so that I could live day to day, but I knew one day you would be mine once more."

He embraced me fiercely.

"I'm just so overwhelmed." He breathed "You're scent, its everywhere, it's imprinted in my head. It's like I can't live without you."

"Well, we need to get to this meeting. I need to explain everything properly then I'll head out to see Kilvire."

He growled a response.

"Vincent I have to go. You would not be here were it not for him."

"I am coming with you, do not even argue woman."

Chapter Fifteen

"I'm coming with you." Robin claimed.

I had brought everyone up to speed and then gone on to explain about my summoning by Kilvire.

"Robin, you are not."

"Like hell!"

"Do I have to pull rank… really?" I said

"Erm last time I checked, Vinnie ran the show."

Darn, she had me there. I turned to Vinnie, pleaded with my eyes.

"We'll take her Ginetta, she is stronger than I." He replied.

"Vincent!"

"If she goes I go." Red piped up

"Son, no." Ilona replied

"I'll be fine mum."

"Then I go too," Ilona said defiantly

"Me too." Her mate, Redvick added.

"For Christ sake. It's not a family holiday." I nearly yelled.

"Ginetta, chill," Robin said, "you know your fucking problem. You don't rely on others when you damn well should."

I was silent.

"We love you," She continued, "Vinnie, evidently more than any of us. The point is we aren't going to let you wander off and have tea with a mad bastard of a vampire."

"Nicely put," Horaldo who had been silent spoke. "I too will accompany you. I insist."

It was done I was seriously out voted.

We took Vinnie's private plane and booked in at the same hotel. I knew as soon as our tires set down on Tibetan soil Kilvire would know I was there. He would know my thoughts and he would know I had company. Part of me was glad to have everyone with me, the other half was scared.

I wasted no time in asking Lance to organize our passage.

"I must say I am surprised to see you return, glutton for punishment are we?"

"Just business." I replied quickly.

Vincent booked us the best suite in the hotel of course. Even went as far as ordering a bottle of the freshest blood from a bottle.

"You hate drinking it like that."

"The funniest thing happened. When Malachi sent one of his ladies round for me to feed on, it was strange."

"Strange?"

"I mean I have always liked to… you know"

"I know, I've been there, remember?" I laughed softly.

"The best years of my existence were with you."

"I was feeding and, well the blood tasted the same but the rush wasn't there. All I could think of was you."

I smiled, my heart soared at the words I had longed to hear for so long.

The hotel room was lush to say the least. A lovely roaring fire crackled away merrily at the end of the bed. We stood side by side at the window and looked out at the spectacular view of the mountains.

"What is he like now Gina?"

"Kilvire?"

"Who else."

"He is scary. In all honesty I thought he was going to kill me. How did you meet him?"

"I was young, only turned for maybe a year, I was hunting and I saw him ransacking a village. He was like a disease, flashing to the huts of the villagers so fast, killing everyone in his wake. I only survive because I had the sense to haul ass. There have been many rumors of his madness over the millennia. It would not surprise me if they were all true."

"I am not looking forward to a second meeting but in all honestly I cannot say no."

"I know. We will face him together, let us hope he doesn't want his ring back." He chuckled.

He embraced me and breathed in the scent of my hair.

"You smell like orange blossom."

"It's my shampoo." I laughed.

"It reminds me of that first time I saw you. You were so young, so vulnerable. On your way back to Collette."

"That wasn't the first time we met"

"Of course, I'm sorry I cannot remember that."

"Collette was not too bad. I wonder what became of Anazia, I like her."

"Your friend, at The Gilded swan?"

"Yes, without her I wouldn't…" I held my tongue

"Wouldn't what?"

"Nothing." I said quickly

"Oh come, no secrets between soul mates."

"Vincent, when I officially joined your harem, did you not wonder why I was so experienced all of a sudden?"

"I did!"

"Anazia served her time at the Gilded Swan but decided to stay on. She was the highest paid there and had a Roman suitor. She erm gave me a few pointers."

"Did she teach you how to do that thing with your tongue?"

"Vincent!"

"What? I'm just asking. Well did she?"

"Yes. We even made out too, she said I should have told you that, that it would have drove you insane."

"So you are telling me that instead of staying with your mom you were at the highest paid brothel in town getting sex tips from a beautiful woman and you kissed her?"

"Don't say it like that, I had no choice. I had never even kissed a man before you. I knew nothing and I was scared you would quickly tire of me if I were inadequate.

"Wow, if I had known we could have…"

I slapped him playfully.

He winked at me.

"It's been a while since you did that particular trick." He took my hand and guided it to his pants. I smiled wickedly at his member, ramrod stiff. "Hmm, that's me just thinking about it you and another woman."

I smiled, unzipped his trousers and sank to my knees.

The same vampires led us up the mountain. We set off as soon as the sun disappeared behind the mountaintops. Despite my fear and reservation, I was less afraid having all my friends so close to me. Robin complained that she was ruining her new *Ugg* boots. I didn't think that was a bad thing as they looked to me like old lady bootie slippers only they went up to her knees. Apparently they were in fashion.

Ilona and her mate Redvick stayed near the back. It had been hard for Ilona to fly and she wasn't used to being in strange places but she was determined not to let Red, her son out of her sight. Horaldo walked with Robin and Red chatting away. Vincent walked alongside me, deep in thought.

We camped again during the day, this time finding a well-shaded spot against the mountain.

Vincent and I had our own tent and we lay side by side curled up.

'*Welcome back Gina.*'

I gasped and jumped up.

"What is it?" Vincent said suddenly.

"Did you hear that?" I whispered hoarsely.

"Hear what?"

"Kilvire"

'*Listen Carefully Ginetta, your group is in great danger.*'

I put my hand up to indicate that Vincent should be quiet a moment.

"*Your guides have been paid to kill you.*"

"No." I whispered.

"*They are now waiting for you to be asleep so that they can act. This spot was chosen so they could do it during the day.*"

"Can you tell Robin?"

"*I can only communicate telepathically with those I have been in close proximity to.*"

"What do I do?"

"*Go now, take Vincent and tell your Santorian. Guard yourself.*"

"I don't know the way, they are our guides"

"*Worry not, I will guide you. Go*"

I nodded and then told Vincent. We unzipped our tent. There was no sign of anyone. I winced at the daylight but in the shady spot it was relatively safe.

I ran over to the other larger tent that housed Red, Robin, Redvick, Ilona and Horaldo. I unzipped the door and quickly stepped in.

Robin was snuggled up to Red. Ilona and Redvick were at the other end and Horaldo was fast asleep in his own sleeping bag with his back turned away from us.

"Ginetta what is?" Robin said.

Robin, being a Santorian didn't feel the need to sleep during the day so she woke up straight away.

I quickly explained.

"So you hear voices in your head telling you somebody is trying to kill you and you decide to kill them first?"

"Ok it sounds crazy, but it's Kilvire."

"He's the craziest loon of all!"

"Look if it's true, they are going to kill us first. There are only two of us in our tent. So we wait, if they make a move, you kill them."

"Me!"

"Three vamps will be no match for your awesome strength." Vincent added.

"Why thanks Vinnie that's… hey wait, when I have to save someone, I get staked!"

"Yes but you get the privilege of surviving that." Vincent said with a wink.

Robin started gently shaking Red awake.

Wc took our leave and made our way back to our tent, aware that we were probably being watched.

We walked side by side, Vincent had his sleeping bag left open so he could jump up and attack. I honestly wanted to be wrong but an hour later we heard the sound of someone treading carefully over the rocks and rough terrain we had set camp on.

My heart sluggishly kicked up a notch. The person then began unzipping the tent door, slowly. Vincent silently rose and as quiet as a mouse picked up a samurai sword from beside our belongings. He crouched in a battle pose, ready to strike.

"What the…" The question was followed by the shrill cry of a man outside and we heard another trying to run away.

"Robin, was that *really* necessary?" It was Red's voice shouting.

Slightly confused Vincent finished opening the tent and we stepped outside. I stepped into something gooey. I was barefoot and I did not want to look down. I did and I wish I hadn't. It was an arm, detached from its owner and I'd stepped in all the sinew and muscle exposed at the end. I screamed as it twitched.

When I composed myself I saw another vampire was missing a head. The owner of the arm was a few feet away, a second glanced told me not quite headless, but almost.

Red stood beside the carnage looking like a highly embarrassed boyfriend, we were all used to Robin. Her temper made her forget her strength sometimes.

We heard a sound of something whizzing through the air. We only had a few seconds to ponder what it might be when a body crashed into our tent, not three feet from where I stood. It was then I noticed Horaldo stood at the entrance to his tent with what could only be described as a look of adoration on his face.

Robin moved so fast it was as if she materialized right next to us.

She hauled the last vampire out of the wreckage that was our tent and dumped him in front of Vincent.

He was only half unconscious but his first words were,

"You will all die."

"Wrong answer dick head," Robin kicked him in the ribs. We heard an ear scrunching noise and the man flew a few feet in the air.

"Robin, calm yourself." Vincent laid his hand on her shoulder. "Nice work but you can calm down now."

Robin's eyes were blazing red, which happened when ever I'd seen her really angry. Once when she missed a handbag sale with a 75% off sale.

The man laughed, winced then tried to laugh once more.

"Who sent you?" Vincent asked him calmly.

"You might as well kill me now, I'm not going to talk."

"Very well, Robin, dinner's up."

"Nice!" She answered like someone had offered her a sandwich instead of a vampire. "You mind if I take him round the back."

Vincent nodded and Robin dragged off the vampire who was still not giving any information in the face of certain death.

We heard a short cry a few seconds later and we looked at each other awkwardly.

Robin reappeared wiping her mouth with the back of her hand.

"Where are the humans?"

I hadn't thought, like my last visit we had brought with us some humans. We looked in the direction of our vampire guides tents.

Vincent took the first step. He approached the tent and unzipped it enough to peer inside.

"Not good." He said poking his head out once more.

"Dead?" I asked.

"Very."

"Great."

Vincent looked at our tent.

"I'll guess we'll bunk with you lot tonight."

We all bedded down. Robin insisted on staying awake. She took her eBook reader out of her backpack and positioned herself outside the tent.

I fell into an uneasy sleep. I was afraid of others coming.

I was relieved when instinct told me the sun had gone down.

Robin was still perched on a rock outside our tent only she was looking a little tired.

"You look awful." I told her.

"Yeah, and I got blood on my *Uggs*." She replied sadly.

On the surface Robin appeared to be a very materialistic and selfish person. She swore, didn't care what she said or whom she said it too. It was true, she adored nice clothes and especially shoes but she had blossomed into the most selfless person I knew.

She was fiercely loyal to the pack; with her strength and abilities she had become an enforcer. She had followed any orders I gave her to the letter even though she was considerably stronger than I.

I had grown very fond of Robin and so had Ilona, surprisingly. The two had really bonded.

"I'm sure Red will buy you more," I laughed.

We collapsed the one remaining large tent and packed what belongings we had. We had four bottles of blood, which, after shaking them up, were just about edible.

Then we stood and waited.

"So what now?" Robin asked.

"Erm, I'm not…"

'Take the compass from the vampire the Santorian fed on.'

"Ok. Robin the vamp you fed from, he has a compass."

"How do you know?"

"Kilvire is telling me."

Robin rolled her eyes but set off in the direction of her victim. She returned a minute later wiping a heavy old-fashioned compass made of thick brass.

"Does anyone have a clue how to use one of these?" She said tilting it back and forth.

"Yes." We all replied at once.

"Oh yeah, I forgot, you are all ancient."

'Listen Carefully, Ginetta of Rome.'

I quieted everyone

'From the point where you are now, head east alongside the mountain'

"That's the opposite direction almost."

"There is passage through the mountain. The terrain is slightly trickier but you are more than capable."

"Erm, OK, Kilvire says to head east"

"Ginetta, it's all mountains east." Vinnie pointed out

"There's a way through, a short cut"

The short cut turned out to be a hidden path winding up and along the mountain. Well, I say path, it was barely a foot wide. We clung like tree monkeys to the side of the mountain and scaled our way along. Ilona was suffering the most. She did not even have the strength of a newborn vampire, or night vision to aid her. She was wedged in between Red and Redvick.

After five hours of balancing and sliding the path began to slope downwards and we found ourselves at the bottom of the rocky path leading to Kilvire's temple.

"Maybe everyone should wait here."

I received various responses, all boiling down to the same thing, *not a chance.*

We made our way up the now familiar path until we reached the archway that led to the grounds of the temple.

"Wow," Robin exclaimed

I led the way up to the huge double wooden doors. I knocked and then eased it open.

My eyes adjusted to the near darkness. Speckles of dust floated through the air and I saw Kilvire sat at the same alter. The seven of us walked slowly towards him. As we reached half way, Kilvires head rose up.

We all stopped, waiting to see if it was safe to approach further.

"Please." He said quietly, indicating with his hand that we should come forward.

Chapter Sixteen

"I hope it's ok that I have company" I asked nervously.

"Yes. I was counting on it actually." He craned his neck and in the silence of the temple we heard the bones in his neck crack.

"Curious" he said softly.

"Kilvire?"

"I knew your Santorian was with you. I could sense her presence but I can only now read her thoughts."

"Kilvire, please could you tell us why you summoned me?"

"There is a great plan underway. In three days a horde of vampires will descend on this temple, their plan is to capture me alive. I know not of their plans in depth, but I do know that after they take me they plan to wipe out the Vampires of Britain."

"Why Britain?" I asked.

"Even I know that your pack is the largest, strongest."

"So you called us here to defend you?" Vinnie interrupted.

"Ah the great Vincent Magnus. I have heard much of your comings and goings over the years. I am not worried about the vampires. Many have tried before and all have failed. Those who have sought the ring from this place have never succeeded, only this time the ring is not the only thing they seek."

"You said they want to kidnap you?" I said. Then I realized there could only be one reason why a horde of vampires would want the oldest vampire on earth. "My god! They have a Santorian."

"It is more dire than that. This pack had been growing in numbers for a while. I have heard of their increase from travelers. Many Vampires make pilgrimage here. When the pack sent members here three weeks ago I sensed that had not one but three Santorians with them."

"Three!" I gasped.

"I probed the minds of those within my reach. Most of them are mere drones. Made to be part of an army and ignorant of fact. However I have been able to gather enough to know that these Santorians were not reborn, they were made."

"Impossible!" Vincent gaped.

"Even I was shocked Vincent, and it has been many years since I have felt such a sensation."

"How?" I continued

"I know not. I have called you here because they plan to take me, and wipe out the more dominant packs. They know you have two Santorians." He paused "Yes I know about Ethan as well. They plan to keep me and use me for food."

"I can't believe there are three more." Robin, who had been unusually quiet, spoke.

"They have only sent three. They have more. I do not know how many, I only know they are trying to create enough that they can over throw the major packs."

"Good Lord," Horaldo said angrily. "How long do we have?"

"Tomorrow at dawn. They will know by now that you have survived their feeble attempt to kill you."

"So at Dawn tomorrow a horde of vampires will descend on this temple and us eight alone must destroy them." Vincent looked caught between horror and excitement.

"The vampires I can take care of, it is the Santorians that I need you to dispose of."

"Sir, my wife will need a safe place." Redvick asked softly.

Kilvire looked at Ilona and she bowed her head as their eyes met. Then she slowly looked back up until their gaze locked once more. Something was going on between them; they were locked in a silent conversation. Ilona's face creased and she absorbed information and then finally she nodded.

"Your wife will be fine Redvick, she is stronger than you think"

Redvick did not answer.

Kilvire closed his eyes and a moment later a door at the back of him opened and in stepped four figures. They were human, three young girls who couldn't have been older than twenty and a man. The girls wore virginal white robes and their black hair hung down their backs. They were beautifully vacant. The man set himself at the foot of the altar and bent down on his knee. The girls did the same, going down on one knee but at the side of the altar.

No one spoke but we all knew that Kilvire must have been giving secret instructions because a moment later the man approached our small group.

"I am Ivan, I will lead you down to the catacombs where we can give you refreshment. I will also show you the weapons chamber."

Vincent and Horaldo visibly perked up.

We walked silently passed Kilvire, following Ivan to the back of the temple.

"Like the sweetest nectar sent from heaven itself." Kilvire said softly.

When we all turned to look in puzzlement he continued

"Your Santorian, she is wondering what it would be like to feed from me?"

"Robin!" I chastised

"What? I was only wondering jeez."

We all looked back around to Kilvire who seemed not annoyed, but amused.

We were taken to the heart of the temple, the catacombs. The air was thick and musty; I wondered how humans could even breathe down there.

Ivan grabbed a torch from the wall and led us deep down a winding stone staircase. It came out at a maze of corridors.

The walls were lined with row upon row of spaces big enough for a body to slot inside.

"This temple once housed the bodies of ancient royalty." Ivan spoke softly. "I will take you to one of the larger chambers where you can rest and the girls will permit you to feed."

"Might we ask you some questions Ivan?" I asked

"The master has permitted me to answer anything you may wish to ask."

We came to a large burial chamber. Torches burned on the outskirts of the large square room. A rough wooden pallet table and two benches sat in one corner and in the other dozens and dozens of furs had been laid on the floor.

"You can rest here."

"Where are you all from?" I asked Ivan. There was something simple about the slightly pale humans before us. True they were stunning each one of them but they seemed almost vacant.

"We are from the surrounding villages. We are sacrifices to Kilvire. Each year our Villages bring a youth and they are left at the temple arch. We are to serve master Kilvire for ten cycles and then we are permitted back to our village. In return he protects us from our enemies."

I was lost for words.

"It has been this way for centuries, ever since Master came to this temple."

"It seems so…"

"I know how it may seem to an outsider…" Ivan answered my question, "the master teaches us, educates us and he rarely feeds now. I have been here four years and he has only fed from me, maybe a dozen times. It is not such a sacrifice when we return to the villages and are almost worshipped ourselves. Do you wish to feed here or in private?"

Ilona and Redvick opted for private, as did Red. Vincent and Horaldo said they were happy to stay. Ivan took the three girls, Ilona, Redvick and Red out of the chamber and a few moments later two more girls and another young man entered.

One approached Horaldo who was seated at the bench. She knelt and placed her hands delicately on his thigh and kept her head down. Horaldo was well accustomed to this kind of feeding and wasted no time in burying his face in the girl's neck.

The remaining girl had knelt at Vincent's feet and the young man had done the same to me.

Vincent took the lead. I could sense his hunger and the temptation of blood was too great.

"Don't mind me," Robin said and sat herself down in the mass of furs.

The young man was absolutely stunning in his youth. His skin had been oiled with what smelt like blossom oil and it reminded me of Rome. His body was slightly pale for a native but he was flawlessly built with each of his muscles clinging to his tapered frame.

Not wanting to prolong it I fed quickly. I didn't take much, I was eager to rest after our long excursion and upcoming battle.

Vincent had finished just as quickly; Horaldo had finished feeding and was delicately kissing his dinner. She responded eagerly.

We joined Robin on the fur throws and I snuggled into Vincent.

Dawn was approaching; I could feel it telling me to sleep.

Ivan returned with the other three Vampires in tow.

"Rest now masters. " He said bowing his head. "I will return an hour from sun down to take you to the weapon store."

The seven of us had more than enough room on the throws and we each lay in silence. We had so much to say, to ask. We didn't know whether the impending battle would see us all surviving. We didn't know how strong the Santorians were in this approaching horde.

I hugged Vincent even closer knowing that with his relish of battle he would be in the thick of danger. I could not bear the thought of losing him all over again.

I forced my mind to empty and closed my eyes. I only managed to drift in and out of sleep. Sometimes I woke to find Vincent clinging on to me in his sleep, softly calling my name.

I didn't know what tomorrow would bring for our little group and I was more scared than I had ever been.

We were all awake well before Ivan came back in. The rough bench housed Horaldo, Vincent and Robin who were exchanging battle stories. I sat with Ilona while Red and Redvick exchanged pleasantries.

It was pretty obvious just by looking round our strange group that the prospect of a good fight was exciting to some, Horaldo, Vincent and Robin and for some was absolutely terrifying, that would be the rest of us.

Vincent had not faced a proper battle for many hundreds of years and he was a warrior at heart. Bred to fight. Horaldo was eager to see Robin in action and Robin was eager to please.

Ilona seemed strangely calm and I wondered what Kilvire had said to her in their silent conversation.

We followed Ivan through the labyrinth of catacombs to another old chamber. This one was lit with very old oil lamps.

"Oh mama!" Vincent gasped.

We all squeezed in and even I had to gasp.

The walls were lined with every weapon you could ever have imagined existed. There were swords, hammers, maces, daggers and lots of strange looking ancient Asian swords. All of them looked like they were newly forged, all shiny and glistening in the light of the oil.

"Vincent…" Horaldo whispered.

"I know," he answered.

"Have you ever seen anything…?"

"No my friend."

I expected them to burst into tears of nostalgia.

Ivan walked into the center of the chamber and pointed to a smaller door on the left hand wall.

"Through there is the battle armor you may…"

He didn't get time to finish. Vincent and Horaldo practically jumped over each other to get to the small entrance. We all laughed and went to see. The room was so full of armor and swords that there was no way anyone else could fit in.

Everyone walked round looking at the various weapons. I had never needed to master weaponry but Vincent had given me some archery lessons so I chose a crossbow.

Ilona surprisingly picked up a bag of throwing knives, I kept my mouth shut.

Red and Redvick both chose slim sinister looking swords.

"We have armor to fit women."

"I have never worn it, it would probably hinder me." I answered

"Yes, me too." Ilona replied.

"Mistress, your weapon of choice?" he addressed Robin.

"Mmm, Samurai swords." She walked over to a particularly nasty looking display and removed the longest and a shorter sword. "Wow."

"Where have all these weapons come from?" I asked

"Some are from battles and some are made. The master teaches us."

"Wow, it's like they're here waiting for a war."

"Some would say, the master knows things."

"About the future?"

"Yes, but none would dare to be so bold as to ask him."

My breath caught as Vincent stepped back in to the main chamber. He was wearing a steel set of armor and was carrying the helmet under his arm. I could see glimpses of chain mail at the gaps in the shoulders. I went weak at the knees. The breastplate was inlaid with intricate Tibetan designs and some strange writing inlaid with gold.

"Close your mouth Ginetta my sweet." He said.

"You look, you look…" He read my mind.

"Perhaps Kilvire will let me take it home, for future use."

Horaldo stepped out behind him. He had chosen a lighter set of armor but looked just as ready for battle.

"To victory!" Vincent cried.

"To Victory!" Horaldo answered. They clanked hands and hugged awkwardly with a crashing of metal.

"Your weapons masters?" Ivan asked them.

"The hammer for me my friend and a short sword." Vincent answered.

"The mace and a short sword for myself." Horaldo followed.

"Might I lead you upstairs now, the master is waiting."

"Of course."

Ivan led the way Vincent and Horaldo followed closely behind clinging and clanging with every step. We were silent now, the impending battle was near and we were all thinking about it.

Kilvire was at his altar as we entered the main chamber. I wondered if he remained there indefinitely.

"Welcome, I trust you fed and slept well?"

"Yes." We answered.

"The group is about thirty minutes due south. You will take position at this side of the arch. I ask that you stay at this side. I cannot protect you the same if you pass through it. I should be able to handle the vampires. If any do manage to reach you they should be able to be dealt with quite easily. There are none over a hundred years old.

The Santorians are another matter. I cannot sense how strong they are and they may be able to reach you with ease. I will do what I can."

We all turned then saw that Kilvire had remained seated.

"I must do my part from here. The movement would distract me; I need to feel their minds. Trust me my friends you will see why."

We had no option but to trust him and plodded down the steps and along to the archway. The wind picked up, blowing my hair and I said a silent prayer to Mars, the god of war to help us, to aid us. I begged that he would allow us to survive this battle where we were horribly out numbered more than ten to one.

Vincent, Horaldo and Robin stood front and center, about ten feet from the arch.

Red and Redvick stood slightly behind and Ilona and I climbed the rocks to get a position for our weapons. Then we waited.

Soon we heard footsteps, many footsteps all in military rhythm. As they rounded the corner and came into view we could see that they could only fit three along the path to the archway. The Vampire in front halted them.

"I see you managed to get here after all." He shouted.

The commander was confident as he addressed us. He wore dark, almost Ninja like clothes and had a head of jet-black hair.

None of us replied.

"We are not interested in you Vampire, it's the ancient one we seek. Stand aside and you may live to see another sunset."

"Christ, don't half fucking drone on, do you?" Robin shouted.

The Vampire was taken aback.

"Your choice is made."

"What the hell did you think, we were all gathered maybe for a fucking tea party or something."

Vincent and Horaldo let out huge belly laughs and even I smirked a little.

The vampire went bright red in the face. He pointed his sword forward and the others swarmed around him. When the first three reached the arch they clutched their hearts and dropped to the ground, the rest stopped. They writhed in agony and then burst into flames.

"He can't burn everyone, charge damn you!" The Commander shouted.

The others hesitated but obviously had no choice. They charged once more. Soon there were a dozen or so vamps groaning on the floor. More piled in on top. Two seemed to have passed through with no effect. Vincent swung at one with his ridiculously huge war hammer and he went flying into the rock face with a sickening crunch. Robin took care of the other one, slicing up from his hip, diagonally to his shoulder. The two halves plopped onto the floor in a pool of blood.

"Oooh… these are sharp!" She exclaimed.

The vampires poured in, dozen after dozen. The ones that Kilvire couldn't mentally burn Robin, Vincent and Horaldo easily took care of. We could finally see the end of the line leading up the mountain; only it seemed Kilvire was weakening. More vampires seemed to be getting through the arch and Red and Redvick joined forces with the front three. I took a shot at one managing to get through the archway and hit him square in the fore head.

Revick was locked in battle with a huge burly vampire. There were clanging swords. I turned to see Redvick on the floor and slow motion the enemy vampire raised his sword above his head.

I swung my crossbow, knowing I probably didn't have the time to save him but then the burly vamp had a knife lodged in the front of his face and he dropped to the ground like a huge sack of potatoes.

I turned to see Ilona, pure rage in her eyes like I had never seen still poised from throwing the knife.

"Nice shot!" I said

"Thank you, my first time." She said sheepishly.

We watched from our position and picked off the ones we could. Ilona seemed intent on guarding her son and soul mate and hit her mark nearly every time when one was in danger.

I concentrated on the archway, picking off the ones Kilvire couldn't reach.

Robin was absolutely amazing to watch. She was like a deadly dancer with her two samurai swords. She had behind her so much force that it seemed she lightly brushed her opponent and limbs were severed.

Vincent seemed to be in trouble, he had three vamps on him at once and I could not get a clear shot to help him. Twice he was hit in the back with a sword. Thank god his armor was seriously robust.

Robin had an opening but rather than run over to aid him she dropped her sword and hugged the mountain beside her. I was puzzled until I saw her rip a huge boulder out of place hold it in one hand like a basket ball and then hurl it in Vincent's direction.

It hit the two vampires at Vincent's front. They disappeared with the hurtling rock and smacked into the mountain several feet away.

Vincent swung his hammer above his head, whirled around and hit the last one on the top of his head. He crumpled to ground as if someone had removed his bones. Vincent then looked at the boulder a few feet away. It had come to a stop leaving a splatter of vampire smoothie mixture on the mountain wall.

Vincent nodded to Robin and on the battle went.

Soon the enemies were gone and the only ones that remained were the Commander and three others stood at the other end of the archway.

"Impressive." He said nonchalantly.

Vincent, Horaldo and Robin, who had taken the brunt of the battle, were covered from head to toe in blood.

"Yeah well come over here and say that you cowardly bastard." Robin yelled.

He gave a slight nod and the three remaining beside him shot through the arch at an impossible speed. One hit Vincent square in the jaw sending him flying ten feet. Another had punched Horaldo in the stomach, and he too went flying. I realized these were the Santorians and they were much stronger than we had thought.

Only Robin remained standing. The Santorian that had tried to hit her had succeeded but it hadn't been hard enough to knock her over.

She looked really, really annoyed.

She raised her sword and in a flash hacked his arm off at the shoulder. The Santorian screamed blue murder.

"Hurts don't it?"

She didn't mess around, in another swipe she had his head off. She caught it before it hit the ground and then lobbed it off the side of the mountain.

Horaldo's Santorian had by now reached him and was pummeling him like a piece of meat. I was firing bows into the Santorian but he wasn't even batting an eyelid. Redvick joined Horaldo and Red helped Vincent who was getting a beating of his own. His hammer was knocked from his grasp in one swipe and it landed at Robin's feet.

She smiled.

Taking the hammer, she began building up speed, swinging it in great big circles at her side. When it was a total blur she ran towards Vincent's Santorian. He looked round at the last minute then he was knocked a staggering forty feet or so in the air. Before he hit the ground, Robin was at Horaldo's side, she grabbed hold of the remaining Santorian by the arm and yanked. It was unexpected and he tumbled slightly. Horaldo saw his opportunity and with all his strength he raised his short sword and brought it down, beheading him.

"Chuck the head, we don't know if they can be mended."

I looked over. The Santorian that has seen the business end of the war hammer had landed with a crunch. Vincent retrieved his weapon and brought it down on the Satorian's face. It made a mushy sound.

'Retrieve the Vampire.'

We all seemed to have heard Kilvires voice in our head's because all but Ilona and I, who were still perched on the mountain, took off through the arch after the remaining vamp that had decided to scoot.

'We need him alive.'

He was dragged back up a few seconds later looking not nearly as confident.

'Bring him inside.'

The air was thick with victory of battle. Ilona and I climbed down and as Robin passed me dragging our prisoner she said.

"Better aim next time Gina."

I was puzzled until she turned and I saw one of my bows stuck in her shoulder blade.

"Oh my god, Robin!" I gasped, "I am so sorry, here let me."

"It's fine, I didn't even feel it."

They dragged the Vampire up the stairs and into the temple.

Kilvire was still at the altar but he was now supporting himself with one hand.

"Well done my friends." He said sounding slightly out of breath. "Now, what to do with you, you cowardly weasel."

"I will tell you nothing!" he spat.

Kilvire laughed.

"*Please* do not tell me that your name is Tabiath. *Please* do not yield to me your secret thoughts."

The Vampire, Tabiath now looked scared.

Kilvire concentrated with his remaining strength. After a few moments he looked up and said to Robin.

"I have all the information I need, if you are hungry you may take him outside."

"What, no, I have more information." Tabiath cried.

"My poor man, I have seen every nasty little act you have committed, as a human and a Vampire. I will admit to being evil but even I have never done the things you have done."

Tabiath opened his eyes even wider in shock.

Robin dragged him towards the exit kicking and screaming.

The remainder of us waited until his screams died out then there was a slightly awkward pause. Kilvire looked like he was just about to speak when the temple door burst open. It was Robin, alone and she looked deathly pale.

"Santorian?" He asked

Robin looked too shocked to answer.

"Robin?" Red placed his hand on her shoulder

"I...he…my god."

"Explain my dear" Horaldo said softly.

"He used to hurt… children." Robin whispered and then she started to cry.

Red wrapped in his arms and she sobbed.

"I am puzzled" Kilvire said. "How did she know?"

"Sometimes, when she feeds, she sees the memories of her victims"

"Interesting. My apologies. Had I known I would have not suggested you feed from him."

Robin composed herself.

"You weren't to know. Can we just get out of here, I want to go home."

"That is a good idea." Kilvire answered. "But Vincent of Rome I must ask one more thing of you."

"Yes Kilvire."

"I ask that I accompany you, I have seen things within Tabiath's memory. Plans are afoot. Big plans. I am not safe here and your pack is in danger too. I will be of better use accompanying you back to England. I ask your permission."

"We are indebted to you Kilvire and you may accompany us. My jet can carry up to twenty people and cargo too."

"I will ready my men and be ready to travel in twenty minutes. My short cut through the mountain will get us back to town in time before sun up, just."

We watched as he stood before us for the first time. He was taller than Vincent but of a much lighter build.

"I want to thank you." Ilona said quietly from the back. "You helped me, guided me and kept my aim true."

"I guided you, yes my dear, however your aim was your own."

"What, but I thought you said…"

"I did indeed say I would help guide your aim. You underestimate yourself Ilona, you do not need to depend on others, and there is strength within you. Use it Ilona, you are not as weak as you think."

"Thank you."

"Let us waste no time. You will find holy water you can use to bathe away the worst of the battle. I will gather some weapons to take with us. Not much, my finer pieces are locked away. Oh, and Vincent?"

"Yes Kilvire."

"Yes, you may keep the suit, battle becomes you my friend."

Chapter Seventeen

Kilvire returned as promised twenty minutes later. He had ten of his followers, five women and five men. They were wearing clothing more apt for mountaineering, which looked really strange after seeing them in their robes.

Kilvire looked very uncomfortable in a pair of khaki pants and hiking boots and a fleece coat.

His minions were each carrying a backpack. The men had weapons and the ladies were compact and looked to be carrying lighter loads.

"Erm Vincent honey, perhaps you and Horaldo should maybe leave the heavy unnecessary armor." I suggested

"No way!" They said together.

"We'll tough it out." Horaldo said puffing his chest out slightly.

"Ok but we didn't just slaughter all those vamps for you to fall off the side of a mountain."

Vincent made a scoffing noise and our strange group left once more.

I thought that Kilvire would lead us back the way we came, through the short cut he had mentally led us through but instead we went part the way then Kilvire rolled a huge boulder in the side of the mountain to one side revealing a very narrow cave entrance.

He waited till we were all inside then sealed it behind us. For a few moments we were plunged into utter darkness. The only sound was the heavy breathing from the humans. Then from behind us, Kilvire lit a torch. He handed it down the line to Vincent at the front and I watched in utter amazement as he picked up another in one hand then with the other hand upturned in front of him he closed his eyes and summoned a ball of fire in his hands and used it to light the torch.

"You would be surprised what gifts great age begets. There is only one way Vincent, if you would like to lead. We walked for around an hour and I was very anxious of the time, I wondered if we would bed down for the night inside the mountain. Just when I starting to become slightly claustrophobic, we came to the other side. The night was lit palely by a large full moon and we found ourselves perched on a small ledge in the side of the mountain. I couldn't see the ground below us but in the distance I could see a neighboring mountain sitting about twenty feet away.

Kilvire made his way to the front and stood on the edge of the cliff. He raised his arms and stretched them out towards the next mountain.

No one spoke. We had seen this Vampire burn another with only his mind, he could summon fire in the palm of his hand. Who knew what other stuff he was capable of? We were about to find out. Without prompting two of his followers came forward and stood at either side of two metal hooks embedded into the mountain edge.

We waited a little longer. Robin looked like she was contemplating speaking, she opened her mouth a couple of times but closed it again. Then we saw it. A rope bridge rising up from the ravine. Kilvire guided it our position and his two followers took hold and hooked it on the ropes.

When it was secure I glanced over to see it ran to the neighboring mountain and was fastened there.

"Wow!" Robin said.

"Thank you." Kilvire replied. "There is a path that hugs this mountain for another hours walk then it descends into the town."

We all looked at each other seeing who would dare cross the flimsy rope bridge first.

Kilvires followers led the way.

"No more than five on the bridge." Kilvire instructed.

We waited until they were safely on solid rock then Vincent and I stepped on next. The bridge bowed, moved under our feet and swayed. Twice I let out a small scream and gripped on tight. I had never been so glad to get my feet back on solid ground.

I looked back to see the rest of our group coming over minus Kivire who waited patiently until we were all safe. We couldn't make out what he was doing; he seemed to be taking a long time. Then out of the darkness he came. Not walking on the bridge, but flying. I say flying it was more like floating. He simply glided across the ravine and he was holding onto the other end of the bridge. He dropped the rope bridge and landed beside me.

"I am the only one that I know of." He said and looked to Vincent.

None of us quite knew what we were letting ourselves in for. The sky was beginning to pale as we finally got into town. Kilvire led the way straight to the cemetery and producing an old iron key he opened the door to a mausoleum.

As I said before I'm a vampire of simple needs. Robin will admit herself to being slightly vain; she loves shoes, bags and a fancy life style. Ilona was a clothes designer and I'd never seen her not wearing high-class fashion straight of the Paris catwalk. I was getting really fed up of sleeping in caves and wandering in dank tunnels, god only knew how they were feeling.

"You do know there is a Vampire Hotel like two streets away." Robin said from the doorway.

"Indeed and there are traitors among them."

"Really? Are you absolutely sure? Because they have hot showers and I think I still have pieces of someone inside my bra."

Ilona choked back some laughter and even Kilvire managed a slight smile.

"Are we really sleeping here?" She whined.

"The depths have been stocked for us and you may feed from my followers."

I'd like to say it was nice but it really was a scene from a cheesy vamp movie. The room below had shelves dug out in the wall to house the coffins of the dead. They were empty of bodies but instead kitted out like bunk beds with fur throws. It was one step away from sleeping in a coffin.

"If I wasn't so exhausted I would go walk about." Robin added.

"It was a good battle." Vincent sighed

"Like the old days." Horaldo added.

"You two, you'd think it was the most fun you'd ever had." I laughed.

"You don't get battles like that anymore." Vincent said seriously. "I remember returning from the battle field to a tavern of wenches and a frothy brew."

"Good times, and you were legendary my friend." Horaldo said.

"For crying out loud!" I clipped Vincent on the back of the head. "Get the bloody armor off and pick a bunk."

All of us had made our way down but as we looked we realized Kilvire had stayed above.

Ivan saw me looking at the stone stairs.

"He sleeps alone, do you wish to feed Mistress Ginetta."

"No I'm fine, Vincent will probably need it to heal."

Ivan nodded at the others who divided themselves up and fed the warriors.

At over two thousand years old I could go a week without feeding if I really needed to.

I looked at Vincent still glowing with rapture from the battle. In all honestly I had never seen him so relaxed since those carefree days back in Rome. I watched as he removed all his armor. Blood stained his clothes were it had seeped through the edges of the metal. He gave Horaldo another battle like punch to the shoulder. Vincent was a lover of everything modern and liked to have the best of the best, but at heart he was an ancient Roman, his heart longed for battle and a warm body waiting to ease his wounds when he returned.

He caught me staring and smiled. I saw pure love within his eyes. He tilted his head, inviting me over. He sat cross-legged on a fur throw and I sat in his lap. I felt his firm thighs encase my lower body. I felt tiny in his embrace. I snugged into his chest, which smelt slightly musty from the battle, but I was content to stay there.

"Are you OK my precious?" He whispered.

"I am, my love. I sense a troubled time ahead." I replied.

"It would seem that you have made us a strong ally though."

"Yes. I hope everyone is fine back at the cavern."

"I am sure. We killed all the vampires in the ambush, this will delay word getting back."

"You seemed invigorated by it. Does it not frighten you Vincent, the fighting."

"Nae, I fought in many human wars. Battle calms the inner beast. I have been a leader of the pack for so long that I had lost sight of the real Vincent. It awoke on the battle field."

"What are you saying?"

"Perhaps when all this is over we should seek excitement Ginetta. See this modern world and all its wonders. I have barely left England for centuries."

"I never thought I would hear you say you wanted to leave the cavern."

"Not leave entirely, but take more of a back seat. I am yearning for excitement, especially now my soul is complete. What say you, my love?"

"I say I will follow you to the ends of the earth, but not smelling like this."

"That, my precious, is the smell of victory!"

"Hmmm well I hope you are not planning many victories in the years to come. I had no idea that a vampire could sweat so much."

Chapter Eighteen

It was a very restless days sleep. We shifted uncomfortably in our slumber knowing we were only one door away from sunlight and that we had many enemies who could very well have been watching. When my instinct told me that the sun was finally setting I felt much relief. Vincent sensed my apprehension. Gone was the adrenaline rush from the previous nights battle and in its place was the impending battles ahead.

Kilvire reappeared and we all readied ourselves to go. Kilvire did not seem to relish the thought of flying in a machine and voiced his opinion several times. His followers, ever silent, merely nodded in agreement. Ivan didn't leave his side.

I on the other hand was never so glad to get my backside on that plane and be up in the air and heading towards home.

We touched down and made our way back to the cavern right away and called an emergency meeting. Malachi was there as well as Elaina and Ethan. We were all eager to hear what Kilvire knew and what he was willing to share.

Vincent ordered fresh blood for us and we were informed that in our absence his apartment, the most luxurious in the pack base had been vacated for his return.

"Excellent, have Ginetta's belongings shipped in as soon as possible."

I opened my mouth to protest, after all I had not been asked but then I closed it again. I knew as well as he that that had been the next move on the table.

Once we all had our nourishment and were comfortable Vincent went over the battle for those that had not been there. He brought us right up to the point where Kilvire had announced that he had information and then all eyes were on him.

Kilvire did not look like his usual sharp self.

"Forgive me," he said slightly strained. "There are a lot of voices nearby, it is difficult to block them out."

"Take your time" Vincent replied.

"I will not be able to stay here." He added. "Do you have another hideout, less populated?"

"We stay in a mansion" Robin offered, "we have staff but I suppose we could give them leave. The grounds are extensive."

"Then might I trouble you to accommodate me?"

"Of course."

"Thank you. I will now tell you what I know. The leader was a little better informed and I have pieced together the pieces enough to work out their methods. They discovered the method of making a Santorian some time ago and I am afraid I suspect they have quite a few in number. I saw in Tabiath's mind a great room with at least a dozen new

Santorians, thirsty for blood and heavily strapped down. I saw cells of bloodthirsty people, newborns.

"Their plans were to capture me and use me to create the ultimate army. Then they planned to capture the older more influential vampires and take over the packs, so that they would be the more dominant presence known on earth.

The method is simple yet complex and the only reason they have great number is they have sacrificed many vampires in the process."

"How is it done?" Vincent asked.

"You take a Vampire and drain them to the point of death then a Santorian feeds them."

"That's seems very… logical." Vincent said with a most puzzled look on his face

"Indeed I saw many vampires in the most terrible states. Animalistic, primal. If the blood doesn't turn them they are driven mad or worse, if too much is drained the vampire dies."

"So similar to a human being turned."

"I guess only from what I saw a much smaller window to get it right"

"So what do we do with this knowledge?" Vincent asked.

"We need to experiment, reinforce ourselves as well."

"Experiment, that's crazy!" I chirped in, "That makes us no better off than those we wish to fight."

"Surely you have to trim the dead flesh from your pack from time to time." He looked at us in a knowing way, after all he had already seen inside everyone's head.

"We have had to dispose of vampires who have betrayed us."

"So instead of killing them you can experiment on them. It's a means to an end."

"And the Santorian blood, I take it you would need us to be willing." Robin asked.

"I need *you* to be willing, this one is not strong enough." He indicated to Ethan.

Ethan, who had been silent all this time, remained so but shifted uncomfortably in his seat.

"I guess we don't have a choice." Vincent sighed, "Elaina, are there any vamps on the shit list?"

"We have one being investigated for theft from the pack and another who we suspect is killing humans but no proof."

Vincent opened his mouth to speak but was interrupted.

"Bring them in," Kilvire said calmly, "I mean, with your permission Vincent, bring them in, I will be able to tell you if they speak the truth."

"Organize it" Vincent directed at Malachi who nodded and rose. "Do you want them brought right away?"

"No we need to set up a lab, organize any lab technicians we have. Pull them out of whatever jobs they hold and bring them here. The medical bay on the ground floor should be big enough. We will need heavy restraints and cells set up."

"Yes Vincent."

Malachi nodded a goodbye to us all and left.

"I can sense your turmoil Vincent."

"I kill when I have to, I always have. It does not rest easy with me experimenting on my own kind."

"Do you want me to head research?"

"Yes, please keep me informed."

"If it will sit easier with you I can bring you the dregs of society, we can turn them to vampires and then experiment."

"Perhaps, let us find out what we are dealing with first."

There followed an awkward silence, broken by Robin stating she was hungry and eager for bed. She didn't speak to Vincent or anyone else but instead stalked out of the room. Red stood and followed, Ilona reached a hand for her son as he passed and he delicately took it, gently squeezed and then let it go.

"Robin is not happy." Kilvire said flatly

"Are you surprised" Elaina spoke. "From what you have said we are facing a war and it rests on her shoulders. She could die couldn't she?"

"I will not lie, some have died, but those have been young Santorians fed only on the blood of young vampires."

In all the centuries since my return to Vincent's side I had never seen Elaina so much as say boo to a goose but she sat with her fists clenched on the table squaring up to possibly the most dangerous creature on the planet.

"So the mighty Kilvire, descends from his shack in the mountains, brings a boat load of trouble and expects our kin to lay down their lives. What will you sacrifice? Will you give your blood to Robin to aid her recovery?"

Kilvire looked as if that were the last thing he had expected her to say.

"Do you know what my blood could do little girl. I cannot even begin to tell you how old I am but humans were practically cave men when I was created. My blood could drive her mad?"

"Could?" Elaina now stood and the rest of us jumped. "She 'could' die, we 'might' succeed, there's a lot riding on if's and maybe's the question remains will you do what you have to do if it will save her?"

"If it will save her, if it is needed, I will?"

Elaina took a deep breath and sat back down. None of us had any idea Elaina felt so passionate about Robin. I wished she could have seen it.

"Subject A. Male Vampire, human age 23 at rebirth, vampire age 42. Convicted of Embezzlement and fraud. Sentenced to death by exposure to sunlight. Sentencing postponed for reason of the experiment."

I watched in awe and horror as Kilvire talked into a small Dictaphone. I pondered how he knew about such technology but it was not the time to ask questions.

A vampire was strapped to the tabled in front of me. We were in the medical bay, which was used to treat out human servants. Two vampire doctors were assisting Kilvire in the first experiment. Vincent was pacing our apartment somewhere above my head.

"I will now proceed to drain 6 pints of blood, totally about 70% of his total blood count. This is the maximum amount of blood a vampire can loose and live. I will monitor internal brain activity myself and if need to will stop sooner."

I don't know why I chose to accompany Kilvire and witness the experiment. Morbid curiosity? I wasn't entirely sure but I knew Vincent would want to know what was going on even if he couldn't be there himself.

Kilvire nodded at the doctors who then proceeded to insert a catheter into the vampires forearm. The vampire was awake but was strapped down and gagged. I couldn't see his face, I was glad of that. I saw the blood leave his arm and travel along the clear medical tube and into a waiting blood bag. It was all being stockpiled in case it was needed later.

The minutes ticked by as the doctors filled one blood bag after the other. Kilvire made notes and now and again laid his hand on the vampire's head. After a while Kilvire raised a hand and the doctors removed the catheter and stemmed the blood flow.

"Go fetch Robin." He ordered me. I had a quick passing thought, a please would have been nice, and then,

"Please." He said with a slight smile.

Red and Robin had a very small modest room in the cavern, which was tiny compared to the apartments. I made my way up the stairs and knocked on their door.

Robin opened it.

"It's time." I said.

Red motioned to follow but she stopped him with one hand motion and a quick shake of her head.

We shut the door and proceeded.

"Are you okay?" I asked her.

"Not really, no one actually asked if I would be willing to do this. I know it's necessary and I know I'm the best candidate but when I was thrust into this whole weird fucked up vampire family I had no idea the lengths I would be expected to go to."

"I know Robin."

"Red is beside himself. He even contemplated running away, leaving everything behind. He has too much honor and loyalty to Vincent."

"And you."

"I will do what is required of me."

We made the rest of the journey in silence and as we reached the medical bay I reached up to push open the steel door, Robin grabbed my wrist.

"If anything should happen to me, you need to take care of Red. You are the only one who knows what he will go through if I am lost."

"You will be fine Robin."

"Promise me?"

"I promise."

We entered.

Kilvire motioned to a medical bed, which had been moved next to the vampire. Robin gave him a look and then made her way over and led down. I followed and took her hand.

Kilvire took her other, pushed her loose sleeve up and wrapped a tourniquet around her forearm. He then inserted a catheter and a clear tube and beginning extracting her blood.

"Robin, do you hate me so much now." Kilvire said softly.

"I do not hate you," she whispered "I know why you are doing this but it seems we risk much for something that might not work."

"It will work my dear, we just have to find the right balance."

"I do not like the idea of being drained and weak, the last time I was short of blood I had my arm hacked off."

"I assure you as soon as I have the amount I need you will be given adequate blood to replenish yourself."

"Peachy."

When the first bag was full Kilvire handed it to his assistant and they hooked it up to the vampire and began feeding it through to his vein as fast as they could.

The process seemed endless.

"Santorian subject is fine, we have now extracted five pints of Santorian blood and I believe this will be a good amount to begin." He nodded at another assistant who opened up a second catheter in the vampires other arm. "From the information I could gather I was able to deduce this, too little and the Santorian blood kills the weakened vampire. The vampire must be drained to the point of death and the Santorian blood must be sufficient enough to replace what is left and kick start the vampire into its new life. Too little and the Santorian blood kills what is left of the vampire's blood but there will not be enough to revive him."

Kilvire nodded to a trolley being wheeled in. There were four large glass beakers filled with blood. I helped Robin to sit up and gave her the first. Her eyes rolled slightly.

"Robin?"

"I'm good."

She gulped down the first beaker of blood and started on the second when the vampire on the table began to shake violently. His back arched up and he screamed behind his gag. The last of the blood was fed into his arms and the assistants and Kilvire stepped back.

Robin watched in amazement.

We saw all the veins on the visible skin of the vampire pop out and bulge hideously. Kilvire continued his commentary.

"All five pints of Santorian blood have now been administered. We are now witnessing the fight between the two bloods. If successful the vampire should go into a sleep state after stage. I will still be able to monitor brain activity and this stage should last around three days after which we should see a rebirth of our new Santorian."

All the while the poor vampire on the table screamed against his restraints, his whole body twitched and shook like he was having a fit and then, just like that he was still.

Kilvire shook his head and laid his hand onto the vampire's head.

"Subject is dead. Zero brain activity. Conclusion, not enough blood administered"

He walked over to the other side of the room and sat at his desk.

"Subject will now be tested to see how much effect the blood administered had. I am surprised that the reaction to the blood was so quick. Note; could the strength of the Santorian affect the speed of the transformation."

Once Robin was steady on her feet we made our way back out.

"Robin you can't do this again." I told her

"I don't think backing out is an option Gina. You know being that there's an army on its way here and all."

"And I gather they will need more blood next time."

I took her not to Red but to an empty apartment near mine and Vinnie's where I sat her down and offered her my wrist. My two thousand year old blood would revive her much quicker than the younger vampire blood. I let her feed until I could feel myself becoming light headed, then I gave her a gentle tap, she looked a lot better.

"Now Red won't throw a complete wobbler when you return to him." I laughed.

"Yes but now you look like warm crap."

"I'm fine, just carry me through to Vincent."

She picked me up and obliged me. Vincent was in his study, pacing.

"Well?" He asked, then. "Christ Gina!"

"I'm fine Vincent, I just helped Robin."

She placed me in one of Vincent's armchairs and left to get me blood.

I gave Vincent the gist of everything that had gone on as best as I could, he did not look very happy.

We were scheduled for the next experiment a fortnight later and by the time it rolled round we were better prepared for it.

Robin had fed well and Vincent had given me instructions to have her brought directly to him so that he could feed her. Kilvire planned to take an extra pint to see if we could get the right dose.

Our victim this time was a female vampire who had fed from a child. She was not a member of our pack but a renegade one we had caught. Her victim had survived, just. She was strapped down heavily to the metal trolley, eyes wide, looking round at us to see if someone, anyone would help her.

Kilvire began speaking into his Dictaphone.

"Subject is female. Human age thought to be mid-thirties, vampire age one hundred and forty. As with previous subject we will drain the subject to the point of death. I will estimate perhaps four pints of blood to be removed as the subject is of a slight build."

He paused and indicated that his assistants should begin.

The medical doors opened behind us and Robin walked in carrying what looked to be a paper cup with a plastic lid and a straw coming through it.

"Robin, how nice to see you." Kilvire said.

"Always a pleasure. So I had this brain wave, maybe. I have here a pint of Vinnie's blood and I thought I could drink it as you take mine."

"A good thought, it would certainly revive you better, take small sips."

She hopped up on an empty trolley and I walked over and stood next to her.

"Are you okay?" I asked

"You know, I am. I'm better, I've had time to get my head around it all. I'm not saying I like it but I don't want to kick the crap out of Kilvire anymore." She smiled

"I would love to see you try, Santorian." Kilvire turned giving her a sly wink. "Well my dear it would seem we are ready for you once more.

"You know we really need to get a T.V. down here, it's far too clinical."

"Robin, it is a laboratory."

"Kilvire, I know but I'm gonna be spending a lot of time in here, I need T.V."

I smiled as she tried to lighten the mood a little. That was Robin, when she was scared or cornered you could guarantee she would come out with some witty line.

They hooked her up. She had her legs up on the trolley and she leaned back on her elbow and sipped her cup of blood with the other. She mmm-ed. To her, Vinnie's blood was the caviar of food.

As the pint bags filled up they removed them and once again began pumping it into the vampires vein.

"As subject is lighter in weight and build than our last I am going to administer the same amount as before, perhaps half a pint extra. Santorian subject appears to be coping better with the addition of the blood she has to hand."

We watched with some impatience as Robin's blood slowly disappeared into the vampire. She lay motionless.

"Brain function is low… according to my recordings previous subject had perished at this point. Brain function the same, lower than average. No thought patterns detected."

He went over to the vampire's head and, using his thumbs open her eyes and then he smiled the biggest smile. Robin and I ran over. The woman's eyes were red, Santorian red.

"Okay, Ginetta you need to leave now, take my two assistant here and send me in humans ones. When this Santorian wakes she will look for vampire blood and we do not want to antagonize her."

I nodded. "I will wait outside should you need me."

I did as he'd asked; I dismissed his assistants and fetched the one human I could find to hand who could assist. It was a young male who had trained as a doctor. He obeyed without question, entering the lab and I waited outside.

I paced a little. I got bored. Then I got really bored. I was just contemplating taking a peek when I heard the most god-awful noise. I could only liken it to a dinosaur movie I watched with Vincent years before. It was like the sound of the T-Rex.

Unable to stop myself I open the door. The vampire was awake and she was screaming, the sound was deafening. Her back was arched with all her weight pushing on her heels and wrists still strapped down. Robin pushed her back down and I looked in horror to see Kilvire with a chunk missing from his cheek.

"Pass me those straps." Robin shouted to the human assistant. He rushed and handed her some trolley straps and she began to fasten them in place around the vampire's middle. Kilvire held her head which thrashing from side to side. I saw they were struggling so I ran, grabbed a strap and tied her legs down at the knees. Suddenly we heard a snapping of metal and in a motion so fast the vampire's arm was free. She grabbed the human and sank her teeth into his hand. Robin was there in half a second but she wasn't for letting go. Then as quickly as the arm had gotten free she was entirely limp. We all looked up to see that Kilvire had snapped her neck.

"Why?" I asked

"Something was not right."

"What do you mean, all Santorians are similar when they are first turned, are they not."

"No my dear. Her brain function was different, working on a lower level, more primal, instinctive. There were no clear thoughts or emotions. I think this was the outcome of an overdose."

Robin stepped around to look at the poor humans hand. A chunk was from the side, deep enough to see bone.

"We better get that patched up." She said.

He nodded but in the next instant dropped to the floor. His body convulsed and he began to foam at the mouth.

Both Robin and I dropped to floor and turned him over. His eyes rolled back into his head.

Kilvire shunted his way in.

"It cannot be…"

"What…" I began, but before I could finish the human sat up straight and looked at us. His eyes were blood red, no whites, and no iris, just red. He let out the same screech that the vampire had and then lunged for me. Robin snapped his neck before he got within a foot.

"OK, what the hell!" Robin shouted. "She bit you too Kilvire."

"I am fine."

"For now!"

"I am fine but I need to run tests and find out why this happened."

"Take a fucking shot in the dark Kilvire!"

Kilvire got up and took a moment to think. I was in shock, I mean I myself had done some crazy stuff the last couple of months to get Vincent back but that was something else.

"I think we gave her too much Santorian blood. She was considerably lighter than the last subject. The overdose dampened her brain function and left it working on a much simpler level. I felt no emotion and no complex thought from her at all. It would seem that the result was a very dangerous creature, as strong as a Santorian but with no thought or reason.

"They looked like Zombies." Robin said.

"In essence that is what she was. It would appear that humans react to it too."

"And you…" I asked

"I feel fine."

His face had healed almost instantly and he looked normal… well normal for him.

"Okay, I think it's time this whole shit idea was terminated." Robin said

"Maybe we should postpone it while I examine the blood. I have never seen anything like this."

By the look on Robins face I think she was expecting a bigger fight from Kilvire, she looked most puzzled.

"Robin I am not so stupid as to deliberately create more of those creatures without us being better equipped for their strength.

"Thank you." Robin replied. "Would you like me to assist you, you know to gather samples?"

"I want to dissect both the human and the vampire, will you be ok with that?"

"Sure will." She answered.

Even though only a few days previous I had performed open-heart surgery I did not want to hang about.

"I will go and inform Vincent of everything." I told them.

"Tell him we will cease the experimenting until I have a better understanding of what happened here."

I had not even made it two feet into Vincent apartment when he pounced on me, leaving no window to explain anything.

His kisses made me forget my purpose. His touch ignited me, awakened me all over again. Some scary stuff had just taken place but soon I was lost, against my will I responded to him vowing to tell him everything… after. It sounds stupid, the seriousness of what had just happened in the lab should have been the priority but we were newly bonded, soul mates and when he touched me my mind totally shut off and the only thing that mattered was feeling Vincent deep inside me.

He had fed while we had been experimenting below and he was full of energy and vigor. Instead of asking for news he gripped me the moment I'd returned home and began to kiss me in the most urgent way. It left me weak at the knees.

"What has brought this on?" I asked, coming up for air.

"Do you remember when you were fifteen and we walked in the orange grove at the villa. The night we picked oranges for May? You picked a blossom from the tree and brought it to your face so gently, inhaling its smell. Then you tucked it into your plait, just at your ear."

"I remember ever second I spent with you Vincent."

"I don't know why I thought of it now, it seems old memories are reawakening with new feelings."

"You were so unreachable, so beautiful."

"I was amazed by your devotion and eagerness to learn and listen to me rambling on about politics and war. I must have bored you to death."

I laughed.

"Okay, I will admit that some of the talks were way above my head, but I listened, the sound of your voice was like a siren calling me home."

"I am home… finally." He smiled and kissed me once more, pulling at my clothes. He was naked except for some black linen pants he sometimes wore to lounge in and watch movies. I pulled at the string on the front and used my forefinger pull on the waistband, loosening the thread so they pooled to the floor. The sight of him bronzed and naked quickened my heart. He scooped me up as though I weighed nothing and without breaking our kiss carried me to our bedroom.

His hands found their familiar contours of my body. He caressed my breast, kneading them gently, teasing the nipples while flashing me that smile. I felt heat rise to my skin and I closed my eyes, welcoming it. I hummed as his mouth covered my nipple, his teeth pierced my flesh and I felt him draw the blood from me.

I arched my back as his hand dipped down, parting me, playing me so masterfully. I hooked one of my legs onto his back giving me leverage to thrust against his hand, showing him how much I needed him.

"You are eager tonight my lovely Gina."

"It's just nice to forget the madness... OH!" I cried as felt my release build. I took a breath and clinched my toes ready for the full force of it. And then it came. I cried out and gripped the sheets below me. He smiled wickedly as the waves slowly ebbed away from me.

Once I had calmed down I explained what had gone on below. Vincent was worried, annoyed but was pleased that Kilvire was seeing sense and stopping the experimentation, at least until we knew what we were dealing with.

"I left him and Robin to it. I would just like to enjoy a couple of days together with no murdering, no weird zombies. Is that too much to ask?" I said while I lazily danced a finger around his nipple.

He hummed a reply and I snuggled in.

Epilogue

I would have been content to lie forever in his arms and forget all the damn nonsense going on around us but a mere hour after I had left the lab there was rapping on our door. I padded through the apartment and opened to find Kilvire with an expression on his face I hadn't seen before… fear.

"What on earth is the matter?" I asked showing him.

"They are here." He said entering the living room.

Vincent had pulled on some pants and was leaning on the back of the sofa.

"Who?" He asked.

"I didn't foresee, I could never have imagined…" We had never seen Kilvire look so out of his comfort zone.

"I can read minds up to around a hundred miles away. That is why I chose my temple where the voices are fewer in number. I don't even know how do begin to describe it Vincent."

"What?" Now Vincent looked worried.

I had gone to Vincent's side and Kilvire approached us.

"One of the leaders of the large pack is here and I was able to read his thoughts, see his memories.

It drains me, but I will show you."

He offered us his hands. We took one apiece hesitantly.

Instantly my mind was bombarded with images of Kilvires life and he seemed to try to focus shifting in a man's face. We were propelled into the man's head and we saw his memories…

We saw ships, cargo type ships laden with large square metal crates. They managed to pull up as close as they could and then with a dozen or so vampires to each one they were carried onto the beach. I saw maybe thirty crates. The vampires opened them and what I saw run out made me cry out. Each crate was packed with the zombie like humans we had created in the lab. They poured out onto the beach like a swarm of wasps and began to run, snarling toward civilization. Kilvire dropped our hands.

"Where is this?" Vincent demanded. "Is it happening now or is this a plan of some description."

"My friend, this is happening now. I was wrong… so wrong. They do not mean to kill the packs of vampires in Britain they mean to wipe out your food source. That was just one lot there. They are dumping these crates up and down the country as we speak and there are far too many for us to fight. They will have reached human populous by now, and in turn each human they attack will be turned in minutes."

"What do we do?" I said in shock.

"You must gather what humans you can and get them to safety. How many humans do you command?"

"Maybe two thousand in all."

"Contact as many as you possibly can, this plague will spread quickly."

"We own a large estate in the highlands of Scotland. It's remote."

"Good, you must begin right away. We must salvage what we can."

There was no time to pack no time to collect my beloved books. Vincent called up every vampire that could drive to take as many humans as they could to the estate. I switched on the T.V in the living room and was shocked to see that already there were reports of the zombies all over Britain. They were advising people to stay indoors and lock their windows and doors. It was something straight out of a movie.

I still had not got my head around all the craziness; I couldn't believe we had gone from thinking that a vampire pack was coming to battle us to the end of the human population of Britain. The more prominent members of our Cavern, Kilvire and his humans were the last to leave. The spread of the disease had not reached us because we were inland. We made our way through the deserted cavern, our voices echoing in the chamber that two hours previous was heaving with life. Vincent had acquired an enormous motor home, we had wanted to fly but air travel had been completely disabled, no one was getting in or out of Britain.

We ambled inside, took our seats and Malachi got behind the wheel. I held fast on to Vincent and when I looked, everyone else was doing the same, Elaina and Ethan, Ilona and Redvick, Red and Robin.

We all looked out of the window saying a last mental goodbye to our home.

Coming Summer 2014
Nila Believes

Chapter 1

I was madder than hell. I stared at my boss, lord how I despised him. His face was alcoholic red, even redder than usual because he was trying not to shout at me. He was also fat, with a podgy, hairy face and a 'stick up my ass' attitude to match.

"You ARE fucking kidding right?" I demanded.

"No I am not Miss Peters and kindly watch your language." he said sternly with a hint of 'I'm scared of this crazy bitch'.

"So some guy gropes my ass, I warn him, he does it again, I tell him to fuck off, and *I* get fired!"

"The man strongly denies…"

"Of course he fucking would, did you see the wedding ring on his damn finger."

"Never the less we can't have customers spoken to like that."

"Listen, what-the-fuck-ever, like I need this two bit shithole job anyway. I'm out of here."

"Don't expect a reference." He retorted as I reached his office door.

I whipped round fast and banged my hand on the door making him shit his pants.

"Don't worry." I said with a smile, "I don't fucking want one, you better hope I don't contact your lovely wife about old Dorothy."

"I… erm… don't know what you mean."

"Really, I saw you humping her in the store cupboard on a crate of beer? Ring any bells. Stuck in my mind because your arse is hairier than your face which I thought would've been impossible but there you go. Have a nice day Mr Stevens."

And with that I left. I took a nice mental picture, click click, of his face, open mouthed staring after me.

God damn it. I'd lost another job and my boyfriend was going to bloody kill me.

'You lose one more job Nila and I swear to god…' I could hear it now.

I pulled my cardigan tightly around myself and walked briskly in the cold night air. Okay I could have handled it better. I'd warned the guy twice not to touch my ass but he was showing off to his friends and, well I can't deny that I do have a nice behind. Sod it! My boyfriend, Kyle was abroad on a training course and wasn't due back for another few days so I figured I would worry about losing my crummy bar job then. I had worked crummy job after crummy job to help pay for all his university fees, I deserved a bit of slack! I picked my mobile out of my bag and rang my best friend, Kirsten.

"Hey girl!"

"Oh my god Nila, have you seen the news?"

"What no, I mean I just finished work… well got fired…"

"Holy shit, you got to get home and turn on your T.V, there's been like thousands of mental patients dumped on the beaches all over Britain."

"Get out, fuck off. Like gibbering idiots all over the beaches?" I giggled.

"No, I'm serious! Stop laughing they are attacking people, thousands and thousands of them. Britain's on lock down. They are saying we've already lost a massive chunk of the armed forces fighting them off."

"You better not be joking. I mean we are in the middle of Britain, nowhere near a damn beach."

"Just get home. You need to get yourself holed up somewhere safe." She hung up without saying goodbye.

Well I'll be. I stopped by the shop and grabbed myself a sandwich and milk for tea, listening out for any news on the sly from the people in there… nothing.

I got home to our little terraced house and switched on the T.V while I took off my shoes and cardie. I clicked on the kettle and flicked with the remote to find a channel that had the news on. I didn't have to flick far every single channel was on an emergency frequency. I was shocked to see Blackpool on the news, which was only made a 40 minute drive away, as the main feature.

We are reporting live from the tower where we have a view of the carnage below. If we look out onto the beach…

The camera panned to the water where there were about a dozen large oblong shipping crates. The camera panned back to the street below and I gasped. *What the fuck!* There were hundreds and hundreds of people running around the streets. You could easily tell the sick ones from their victims. They were impossibly fast. I saw one leap ten feet into the air and land on a woman running. The things looked like… ok I didn't even want to say it out loud… zombies!

These large shipping crates are from an unknown origin and we can only assume that the things inside the crates were manufactured or even bred as some kind of weapon. They are fast, strong yet show little signs of brain activity, almost like they are functioning on instinct. The crates arrived shortly after sunset and upon opening immediately began attacking tourists and locals. Those who survived the attacks are becoming infected within seconds. The government is advising that people board up their houses as best as they can until the government can rescue survivors. We switch now to number 10.

The picture switched to the prime-minister who was looking extremely worried.

We have no idea who has initiated this attack and we are doing everything we can. It is imperative that you board up your windows, lock your doors, if you have an attic take refuge in there as soon as you can. Get as much food as you can and monitor the T.V and radio for all information. We will update everyone as soon as we have an action plan.

Crap, crap crap. Those… things… how long would it take one to get to our town? I grabbed a hold-all from the kitchen cupboard and began piling as much food as I could into it. Thank god I had done the main shop a couple of days previously. God only knew how long I would be stuck in our attic so I opted for non-perishable foods and tins. I packed the kettle, because I absolutely could not survive a zombie apocalypse without coffee. I hauled the bag upstairs pulled down the loft ladders, put the bag up and then looked around for anything else I would need. The loft was floored and we had power and light but it was cold up there so I took up my duvet and electric blanket. I took up my laptop so I could get the news. Then there was an awkward moment. I hoped to god Kyle was safe out of the way. I didn't have parents or family to speak of. I should've phone Kyle's parents but I thought best to get myself holed up in the attic first and call later. And what IF I phoned someone and they were hiding in a cupboard from a zombie. I mean you always see that in movies. I grabbed my Kobo e-reader and a couple of paperbacks and went to my hidey hole. I pulled the loft ladder up behind me, turned on the light and shivered as my breath blew out in puffs in front of me. I laid my Duvet on the floor then the electric blanket and then a sheet. I listened to the street below getting more and more hectic. The sounds of people leaving in the cars, windows being boarded up. Soon the street was in total chaos. We really weren't handling the situation very well. I lay down and wrapped my duvet tightly around myself. I was lonely, I missed kyle, I wished that I could have one person for company. I lay and waited for the longest time. Chalk this up to zombie apocalyptic invasion… night one.

***

I soon grew bored. I wondered idly if it was some sort of huge Joke. I mean Zombies… running around Blackpool? Really. And not just Blackpool, every beach in the UK? It just seemed surreal. I opened the roof window and stood on a box to peak out. Someone nearby was hammering wildly. I had seen one of those things on the news dent a porche like a sheet of tin foil. A bit of ply wood was not going to make a damn difference. After a couple of hours everything was quieter. Eerie with just the odd dog barking to break the silence.

Then I heard it, the front door opening and closing. Footsteps coming up the stairs.

"Nila" A voice called out.

Kyle!

I ran to the hatch, through it open and lowered the ladder. He climbed up.

"Kyle oh my god! What are you doing here?" I threw my arms around him.

"I flew home at dinner but I've been trapped in the airport."

He looked exhausted. His sandy blonde hair was messy. He threw his bag down and hugged me back tightly.

"I didn't know what I would find, if you would even be here or if you'd maybe gone to Kristen's."

"No, I thought about it, but I didn't want to waste time. Did you call your mum?"

"Yes, her and dad are hiding in the cellar."

"Ok, I better switch on the laptop and get some news."

"Cool, you brought the kettle, I have pot noodles in my bag." He opened his large bag and it was filled with all sorts.

"What the…"

"Look the supermarket was a looting ground everyone was grabbing what they could. Survival of the fittest." He gave me a wink and took out two gourmet pot noodles.

I brought up yahoo and god, I soooooo wish I hadn't. There were pictures of these things attacking anything they could get their hands on. Their faces were grotesque. The flesh was grey, dead looking and it seemed that's what they were. Some were missing arms, some had half their faces missing. I felt bile rise in my throat.

I followed the link to the official site which told us that already 75% of Britain was over run in 6 hours. We were being wipcd out. The military were all but gone and the rest of the world were patrolling the seas making sure no one got in or out.

Kyle boiled the Kettle and handed me my noodles, bleugh!

"According to this they will hit this area in the morning." I said. "We have a few hours."

"We should take turns sleeping and drag some of these heavy boxes over the hatch." Kyle suggested.

This was a good plan and after our hearty feast we did just that. I had some boxes filled with books that had never quite made it to a book shelf when we moved in together. It had taken us both to lift them up the ladders.

Then there was nothing to do but wait. We snuggled together under the duvet with the electric blanket on high, well we didn't suppose there would be any need to worry about electric bills, would there.

We pulled shifts, taking an hour each and it was my turn just as dawn was approaching. I took out my kobo and tackled my new Anne Rice book while Kyle, despite the end of Britain situation, was snoring like a baby.

I heard his phone beep within his trousers on the floor and thinking nothing of it I reached in and took the phone out. His mum must be worried about her baby Kyle I chuckled silently.

I can't believe you just left me, without an 'I love you' or anything. How could you! How could you give your last hours on earth to her!

I can recall that moment with perfect clarity even though it happened years ago. I felt a physical pain in my heart, an actual pain. So painful in fact that I clutched my chest and started to hyperventilate. Everything around me was muffled and tuned out, I couldn't focus on anything, I couldn't think past the pain in my chest. I clutched my hand up and rubbed the skin trying to ease it. Part of me wanted to stop there, not to torture myself further by digging up more stuff I didn't want to know. I hit the 'inbox', the messages started the day he 'flew out'

Hi baby, I got your favourite, streaky bacon and breakfast mushrooms for breakfast in bed tomorrow! Can't believe we have a whole week together! Love you loads x

And a few from me telling him I missed him, I was a fool. The next when I pulled up sent a further chill up my spine.

Hurry back with that milk I want your cock again.

I choked and then I looked at the number, how could I not know it, I rang it nearly every day. My boyfriend of seven years and my best friend, Kristen. I began to cry, then I sobbed, great big sobs. Tears rolled down my face as a sagged to the floor.

"Baby?"

I heard his voice, but it sound like he was talking from a distance. I hunched over and sobs racked through my body making my shake uncontrollably.

"Look we will survive this. I mean I've completed all the resident evil games." He laughed trying to lighten the move.

I looked up and shot him a look of pure evil. His phone fell from my grasp and landed on the floor by my feet, screen up with Kirsten's last, lovely message staring up at him.

"Shit." He whispered.

"How could you?" I sobbed.

"It meant nothing Nila, nothing, I'm here, as soon as the shit hit the fan I had to get to you."

"OH PLEASE! Am I supposed to be grateful? I hate you!"

"You don't mean that." He said with hurt in eyes.

"Oh I do, it's over. Go back to your fucking whore!"

"I don't want her, it's you, I was stupid and reckless and I'm sorry. You work such long…"

I punched him square in the jaw and he hit the deck. He groaned and started to get back up.

"Don't you fucking blame me!" I screamed.

"Nila! Zombies for fuck sake."

"Who gives a ripe shit! I have dedicated the last seven years to you Kyle, I've supported you with one crummy ass job after another while you studied and climbed your way up to the job you have today. You fucking cock-end! I can't believe I am stuck here with you. God-damn it!"

I kicked a nearby box in frustration.

"Nila…"

"Don't talk to me… don't talk to me you fucking loser." I got up and went to the other side of the room and switched on the laptop."

I concentrated on my task, tried to forget about the mental images being conjured up in my head. Kristen and Kyle, I hoped they'd be fucking happy together… twats!

A shocking news report temporarily captured my attention.

A news reporter was broadcasting from what looked to be a bunker.

"A new discovery, a few minutes before dawn these creatures looked for retreat. The military was able to un-hole a few and we discovered that they are allergic to sun light. The following video was captured."

The screen flicked to a very shaking hand held camera filming in a street. Three soldiers gathered round the boot of a car. One bravely popped it open. The creature inside bellowed as light hit it and it leapt out and went to attack the men. Its skin burst into flames and it screamed the worst possible noise you could ever imagine. Kyle had come over and was peeking over my shoulder.

"They burst into flames in the sun?"

"Yes, it's a pity you fucking don't." I said with as much venom as I could.

www.ingramcontent.com/pod-product-compliance
Lightning Source LLC
Chambersburg PA
CBHW051502030726
47592CB00006B/2060